What's Bred in the Bone is an exciting, highly imaginative science fiction thriller and police procedural. Whether human or canine, Gephardt knows her characters and breathes life into them. Her writing is taut, the plot intricate and fast-paced. This novel is a dog-lover's dream!
--**Robin Wayne Bailey, author of the** *Brothers of the Dragon* **Series**

There were so many things to love about this book . . . besides from all the animal goodness, there is a good mystery going on. I think this can best be described as a police procedural in space - and with dogs. There's plenty of action and intrigue to keep the reader's attention.
--**Booker T's Farm**

Gephardt does a fantastic job of putting us inside of these animals' heads. Every action they take makes sense for an animal, and you get the feeling that she truly understands what makes our canine friends tick. She also has a great sense of humor, with some pages making me giggle as I read them.
--**Dogpatch Press**

I found the story absorbing and I wanted to keep reading; the day I read it, our dinner was 45 minutes late because I didn't want to put the book down.
--**Amazon Review**

I really enjoyed this book. I stayed up way too late several nights as I wanted to read "one more chapter." The storyline was interesting, and I will be looking forward to other books in this trilogy.

Drawing on deep research into canine behavior, animal cognition, and sustainable environmental design, Gephardt gives us a world full of honor, intrigue, and betrayal, peopled with a cast of believable characters—both human and XK9—we care about, and enjoy spending time with, and filled with problems that are definitely worth talking about.

Please follow **Jan S. Gephardt** on your favorite online platform. She's on Facebook, Twitter, and LinkedIn. Her website https://jansgephardt.com/ includes her regularly-updated blog "Artdog Adventures."

Learn more about **Weird Sisters Publishing LLC** at https://weirdsisterspublishing.com/. The website features "The Weird Blog," and information about all of their book and story releases, from **Jan S. Gephardt**, **G. S. Norwood**, and eventually **Warren C. Norwood**.

THE OTHER SIDE OF FEAR

A NOVELLA ABOUT THE XK9S

JAN S. GEPHARDT

WEIRD SISTERS
PUBLISHING LLC

This is a work of fiction. Characters, names, places, and situations are all from the author's imagination. Any resemblance to actual persons living or dead, organizations, locations, business establishments, or other entities is entirely coincidental.

The Other Side of Fear, A Novella about the XK9s

© 2020 by Jan S. Gephardt

Cover art © 2020 by Lucy A. Synk

Excerpt from *What's Bred in the Bone* © 2019-2020 by Jan S. Gephardt

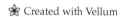 Created with Vellum

For Dora Furlong,
Dear friend and ruthless editor.
What would I do without you?

THE OTHER SIDE OF FEAR

By Jan S. Gephardt

Chapter 1

PLANET-BOUND

"Wake up. Today, you head planetside." The voice of Pamela Gómez's brain implant reverberated through her skull. "Wake up. Today, you head planetside."

Exhaustion sucked her deeper into her nest of sheets, drew her toward the sweet warmth of Balchu's body next to hers. Had she finally slept after all?

"Wake up. Today, you head planetside," the alarm feature persisted. "Wake up. Today, you head planetside."

She pushed herself upright with a groan. Sitting or standing up was the only way to toggle the damned alarm off. *Planetside. This day actually came.*

Balchu's warm caress almost seduced her back under the covers.

She shook her head. "Uhn-uh. Can't."

He sighed, then sat up with a groan of his own and eyed her. He didn't have to say anything. All the words they'd already said hung around them like a cloud of angry ghosts.

Pam lurched up. Padded the few steps to the kitchen. She inserted her mug, and their coffeepot dispensed a blurt of inky liquid. Few candidates were acclimatized to micrograv, so they'd been warned to eat little or no breakfast till they were underway in the shuttle. Not that she was hungry. She sipped the scalding brew. It helped keep her eyes open. Too bad it couldn't thaw the ice in her gut.

Balchu finished in the bathroom quickly.

She filled another cup. Extended it to him when he joined her in the kitchen.

He thwarted her intended clean hand-off with a grasp that engulfed both her fingers and his mug. He relinquished them only after he'd given the back of her hand a kiss.

She bit her lip and pulled free.

With leaden limbs and brick fingers, she packed final items. Seal-locked her Department-issue duffel, then dragged it into their small, threadbare living room. The rancid oil smell from the Ultra-Fast Tempura Shop downstairs hung thicker in here.

Balchu slung the heavy duffel over his shoulder without asking.

She could carry that herself. She almost said so, but she didn't *want* to carry that herself. "Thank you."

His dark eyes regarded her from beneath thick black eyebrows. He opened his mouth as if to speak, then closed it again and shook his head.

She grimaced. *Thank you for not saying 'please stay' one more time. Too late now.* The need to leave him for a month or more had been one of the larger obstacles for her, despite all the fighting they'd done recently.

Idiot girl, Mother's voice chided, an unwanted mental warden encamped in the back of her skull. *You got attached. That's a fool's game!* The words stung as much now as the day Mother'd learned Pam was living with Balchu. Pam took a long, slow breath. *Now is now. What is, is. Foolish or not, here I am.*

One stride brought Balchu to the door. He looked back, inhaled as if he meant to speak, then shook his head again and pushed the door open.

Pam followed. *Yes, I know. XK9s are huge dogs.* "the size of a damned *pony*," he'd said, during one of their arguments. He wasn't wrong. Even though it meant a promotion from Patrol to Detective First Level, the bump in her pay wouldn't rent a bigger place. *If* she was Chosen. Which was a big "if." She shook her head, heartsick. *Not likely.*

Applying for this had started the same way she'd ended up in the Police Academy. *What if? Wouldn't it be interesting? I could be someone special.* Back then, she'd dared herself to apply, in part because Mother would hate it *so much.* Then she'd discovered she really was pretty good. Good enough to graduate in the upper third of her cadet class.

She and Balchu *pang-pang-panged* down the metal stairs to street level, then tramped through mist-shrouded predawn neighborhood blocks. The XK9 cadre was a reach, a challenge, another self-dare. She'd never had a dog. Mother wouldn't even discuss it. She and Balchu couldn't afford one. But all her life she'd wished for one. Dogs always seemed so happy to be with their people, so accepting.

Unlike Balchu this morning. He strode forward, back bowed by the weight of her duffel. His silence pressed down on her like a rebuke.

She scowled at him. "You know if you really didn't want this, you could've told the truth on the Family Acceptance form." The Orangeboro Police Department didn't want to place an insanely-expensive XK9 into an unwelcoming home environment. Balchu must've lied his ass off to keep her in the running.

He marched through the mist, head down. "I didn't want it to be my fault, if you washed out."

He could lose his job as a Detective Second Level with the Vice Unit, if the OPD found out he'd lied. The thick fog chilled her. She walked faster. "Are you sorry I didn't wash out?"

No answer.

The coffee she'd drunk turned to acid in her gut. "Did you secretly *expect* me to fail?"

His broad shoulders slumped. "Don't do that. Not today."

The duffel's strap slid. He caught it, hitched it higher with a frown. "I just—oh, hell. It'll be whatever it is." He tromped away into the fog.

"Balchu!" She hurried after him. He didn't slow or look back.

The commuter terminal lay ahead, an island of brighter mist in the steadily-lightening morning. All three tiers of candidates must report to Orangeboro Grand Central Terminal by 05:30.

Balchu halted at the edge of Central Plaza. He stared toward the terminal.

She stopped beside him. Grand Central was the borough's primary transportation hub. Always busy, it usually wasn't *this* busy, this early. She glanced up at his face, harsh with glare and shadows.

"I guess this is it, then." He let out a long breath.

"Guess so." She swallowed against a pit-of-the-stomach drop. "Can we not part angry?"

"Yeah, let's not." He bowed his head. "I'm gonna miss you." Emotion roughened his voice.

Her throat tightened. "Me too. Miss you already." They hesitated a moment longer, silent. Then Pam took a deep breath and plunged forward.

Easy to spot the other candidates in the crowd. Like her, they wore plain blue Safety Services jumpsuits. Like her, each had just one overstuffed duffel for their personal gear. But the crowd on the elevator platform was far bigger than just the other twenty-nine XK9-partner candidates. It looked as if everyone's entire extended family had come to see them off. Her only "family" present was Balchu.

As if Mother would come for something like this.

Pretty much everybody else's mothers were out in force, though. Also, their fathers. And their aunties, uncles, cousins, lovers, nieces, nephews, and grandparents. She even spotted a few dogs on leashes, or smaller ones in people's arms. Of course, the dog lovers would jump at this opportunity.

Longing ached through her. All her life, she'd watched other people's families and wondered from afar.

They all looked alike. Sure, costumes, ages, and skin pigmentations varied, but every family member hovered near their candidate. Voices chattered in hopeful, anxious, affectionate tones. Brows pinched with loving concern, an expression she'd never witnessed from Mother. Hugs, kisses, hands held, images captured . . . she turned away. Her throat ached. How would that *feel*, to be surrounded with love?

No family is as happy as it looks, girlie, Mother's voice snapped from the back of her mind. Her vision flooded.

Balchu's hard expression softened. He lowered his head, put his arm around her.

She clung to him, cold inside. Would they—as a couple—survive this separation?

You're better off traveling light, Mother always said. *Men leave. Who needs them?*

But who was leaving, now? Pam wrapped her arms around Balchu, pressed her face against his chest. He held her, but said nothing.

At last, Pam pulled back and blinked hard. Then she stared at the other candidates' families, her voice too constricted to speak.

Don't you fall for it, Mother's voice warned. *Love is an illusion. It's a trap.*

Illusion or not, those loving gestures and fond faces presented a beautiful vision. Of course, glamour and illusion were the nature of traps, weren't they? Doubt shuddered through her.

Balchu drew her closer. His solid warmth steadied her. Was that an illusion, too?

Oh, God, here it comes. Pam drew in a quick breath.

Balchu's hand squeezed hers in reassurance.

The commuter elevator arrived with pulses of blinking, multicolored lights and a high-pitched *ding-ding-ding-ding*.

All around them, voices babbled louder in a flurry of last-minute farewells. The candidates would travel to the Hub, then embark from Rana Habitat Space Station via shuttle. After 23 hours, they'd land in Solara City, capital of the Republic of Transmondia, on Planet Chayko.

The doors parted. Pam clung to Balchu for one more full-body hug, one final, lingering kiss. Then she hefted her duffel—well, made it halfway up. Balchu's hand under hers helped her settle the strap on her shoulder. For pity's sake, what had she packed in there, the kitchen sink? Plus, maybe a couple of anvils?

Blue-clad candidates separated themselves from their families.

Pam took a place in line, her throat tight.

The candidate in front of her was a tall, elegant blonde with a short, expensive haircut. Oh. Right. Ashley, or something like that. Pam stifled a shiver. *There's my competition.* Ashlynn-or-whatever had taken one of the qualification tests when Pam did, a formwork exam on canine health and care. The woman finished first out of the eleven who'd showed up. She'd submitted her form with a *beep* of the testing center's pad, stood with a nod to the proctor, then departed with a smug little smile on her face. All of this, before Pam made it halfway through the 100 questions. No big shock *she* was here. Probably a Tier One.

Her stomach twisted in an icy knot. *I must be out of my mind.* Maybe this really was a bad idea. Maybe she should just . . . *no.* Pam clenched her jaws and squared her shoulders. She might be a lowly Tier Three, but she'd made a commitment, and she'd made the cut. Might not have a chance in hell, but she meant to take her shot.

A moment later her head came up at a familiar laugh. She turned to look behind.

Several people back from her in line, four young men about her age clustered together.

"*How misty was it?*" one of them demanded. Ben, from his bass rumble. She'd met these guys at the obstacle-course part of the testing.

"It was *so misty* I thought I'd have to wear swim fins." Pretty sure that was Terry, Ben's patrol partner.

"It was *so misty* my auto-nav couldn't find the switchbacks." That nasal tenor definitely belonged to Tim, Terry's roommate-with-benefits.

"It was *so misty* I . . . ," Berwyn stopped.

"I can't *hear* you," Ben sang.

"Don't leave us hangin', man!" Tim cried.

Berwyn groaned. "It was *so misty* my head got full of fog and I can't think of one."

The other three replied with moans and guffaws, but Pam sympathized. She couldn't think of one either.

Tim, Terry, and Ben heaped laughing insults upon Berwyn, but their horseplay contained no hostility or disdain. This was how the self-styled "Four Amigos" had razzed and cheered each other through the grueling obstacle course.

They hadn't acted menacing, like some of the more cut-throat competitors who'd vied for a place in this candidate group. She'd stayed close to them for safety, but watching them and listening in also lifted Pam's spirits. They'd vicariously encouraged her, too. Now she waved at them. "Hi, guys. Good to see you again."

"Hey, it's Pam! You made it!"

Wow. They'd remembered her. She let a few other candidates move past her so the young men could draw even with her. Terry gave her a toothy grin and a high-five. He was tall, tan, and surprisingly strong. "Congrats! Ben and I are Tier Threes, Tim's a Tier Two, and we're all officially jealous of that rat, Berwyn. He's a lofty Tier One. Can you believe it?"

"Maybe that's why he's so slow-witted this morning. He used it all up on the exams," Tim said.

"Haw-haw," Berwyn answered. "Better to be slow now than then." He focused on Pam. "Seriously, way to go, getting in."

Pam smiled, warmed but still wary of taking things for granted. "Tier Three, but at least I made it. Congrats back at you."

"Yes, yes, it's an honor just to be nominated," stocky, dark-skinned Ben said. "We figure it'll be Berwyn who attracts a dog. He's got that animal magnetism."

Berwyn turned to Terry. *"Don't* let him start barking again!"

Ben laughed. "Arf-arf! Woof-woof! Aroo-oo-oo!" But he muted his sound level. They'd drawn near the commuter-elevator's doors. One of the OPD supervisors leveled an unamused scowl at them. They quieted, but Pam didn't miss the glint of mischief in their eyes and the humorous quirks of their mouths.

Two Uniformed Peace Officers stood just to the right and left inside the big commuter car's entrance. Candidates handed their duffels to one or the other. The UPOs placed the identical duffels into neat rows with methodical care.

Pam moved farther inside, but stayed near the Four Amigos. Harder to be gloomy next to their high spirits, even if they *were* studiously behaving themselves for now.

The elevator took almost an hour to get to the Hub. Fifteen kilometers stretched between the air pressure in the 1-G habitat wheel and the Alliance Standard pressurization for Vertebrate Oxygen-Breathers in the microgravity at the Hub. Pam hadn't been to the Hub in a year, but like all Ranans, she'd learned the basics of moving in micrograv at age 10. All Safety Services personnel continued to maintain basic Class-A certifications with biennial refreshers "up top."

From the Topside Terminal, transit to the shuttle was stupid-easy by design, for a lower attrition rate among tourists. Candidates pulled themselves along a short, marked half-pipe with a handrail. At the end they swung onto a waiting Multi-Passenger Terminal Shuttle, or MUPATS, which some people insisted on calling a "muppet." She gave up her slot on the first one, so Tim could ride with the other three. The Amigos thanked her and waved. Then they jetted away on a burst of retros.

Back to icy solitude. She bit her lip and resisted the low-level nausea that was a given in micrograv.

The next shuttle had open slots on the back row. She grabbed one. *Oh, how special was this?* She'd ended up next to Ashra-or-whatever again. In micrograv, her formerly-sleek blonde hair stood straight out on end in all directions. The woman gave Pam a cold, grumpy stare, then pointedly looked elsewhere.

Yeah, nice to see you, too. Pam scowled toward her feet.

But a moment later, a man about Balchu's age and height took the slot on her other side.

Mmm-*mm*, he certainly improved the local scenery. She took a moment to appreciate his athletic build, the warm bronze of his skin, and the classic symmetry of his face. She smiled at him, glad for a distraction. She'd spotted him on the far side of the room at one of the lectures she'd attended, but they'd never spoken.

He offered her a little nod and strapped in, but his well-manicured hands shook.

Concern crowded out her pleasure. "Are you all right?"

He released a soft, shuddery breath. "Micrograv. It'll pass when we hit gravity again."

"Is there . . . anything I can do to help?" She gave him a sharp look. His skin had gone kind of ashy.

He bowed his head. "Nothing, really. I just . . . I won't be good at small talk."

"Okay." She eyed him, still uncertain. Clearly, she could have it worse, but, somehow, she didn't feel any less out-of-place. Must've stumbled into the row reserved for beautiful people with problems. "Um, good luck."

At least the transit to the gate ended quickly. She'd half-dreaded a bare-bones military shuttle, but *oh, thank goodness.* The OPD had chartered a tourist-class craft. Wrap-around screens dominated the oval-shaped cabin's walls. Crystal-clear images of the sensors' outside view surrounded them. *Smooth!*

She reconnected with the Four Amigos and buckled in next to Berwyn on a padded travel couch. On the forward screen, the view centered on a tiny blue, green, and rusty-red planet, partially obscured by the white swirls of clouds. Planet Chayko, the only other planet within Alliance Space that humans had been allowed to claim besides their homeworld, Earth.

If only Balchu were here. They'd dreamed of traveling together to exotic places, but neither had ventured farther than the Hub or Monteverde, the next borough leeward from Orangeboro.

You're better off traveling light, Mother's voice scolded from the back of her mind. A stupid tear pooled in her eye. She brushed it away, but that just created a little cloud of tiny, hovering droplets. *Crap!* She struggled to cup them in her hand, then push them against the semi-absorbent fabric of her jumpsuit. *No more crying!*

The screens on Pam's left showed parts of two other green-and-white shuttles in the Wayland Transit fleet, with just a glimpse of Wheel One and Pam's own home, Wheel Two, counter-rotating beyond the shuttles. Where in that wheel was Balchu now? The chronometer on her implant's Heads-Up Display told her his day-watch had started. Maybe today he'd find more leads for his trafficking case.

Longing constricted her chest. *No. Must focus. Be here now.* The screens on her right showed a long expanse of Hub and more docks. In the middle-background, Wheels Three and Four counter-rotated. She squinted against the dazzle of harsh light and consciously calmed her breathing till the ache in her chest eased up. She'd seen pictures, but never witnessed this view for herself before. Somewhere *way down there* lay more Wheels. There were eight in all.

The shuttle filled with her fellow candidates. Pam spotted

many she'd seen at various tests or group instruction sessions. A few smiled or waved back, but no one spoke. The old ice-walls locked in. Why should any of them talk to her? *Yeah, yeah, wah-wah,* Mother's voice mocked from her back-brain.

Pam listened to the Amigos' repartee, desperate for distraction. They stayed intent on each other, but it was pretty funny to listen to. Familiar, cold loneliness settled over her. *What would it feel like to be fully included?*

A woman's voice came over the PA. She introduced herself as their captain, welcomed them aboard, and urged them to make sure they were securely buckled in. "We have been cleared for launch," she said.

Excitement rippled up Pam's back, raising hairs along the way. *Launch. Oh, wow. Here we go!*

Rana Station slipped away from the side-screens' view. Velvet black, speckled with stars, replaced it. Half-grav settled over the cabin. The front screen showed a split view: Rana Station loomed large in one half. In the other, Planet Chayko looked like a grape that could fit in her palm. Attendants circulated, distributing breakfast bulbs with hot scrambled eggs or oatmeal, fruit, and drink options.

The 23-hour journey had begun.

Chapter 2

ACCLIMATIZATION

The shuttle's cabin lights brightened. Pam's joints creaked as if she'd held each one in an odd position too long. Her wrinkled, gamey jumpsuit bunched in uncomfortable folds. Her head pounded. *Ugh. Why did this seem like a good idea?*

All around her, people stirred. *Better hustle! There'll be long lines for the hygiene closets.* Even in half-grav her loggy limbs fumbled. Every fiber yearned for her nest of sheets and Balchu's delicious embrace back home. Instead she'd dreamed of falling helpless through chilly darkness. Startled awake over and over by strangers' snores, each time she sank back into gluey exhaustion. And dreamed again of a headlong plummet.

Nothing good comes of space travel, Mother always said. Pam gave a soft groan. *Didn't need that lecture the first time. Don't need to rehearse it now.* She waited for one of the five hygiene closets, her stomach an icy pit. Half-grav made her face puffy. Her hair, longer and darker than Ash-woman's, exploded from its hair-tie and tangled everywhere. No breakfast came.

Chayko's bulk, swirled with clouds, now filled their cabin's front and side screens. Rana's image must've diminished to nothing and closed while they slept. All at once the screens darkened, and the cabin lights rose. *Must've hit the mesosphere.* Pam rubbed her gritty eyes. *Just as well the screens are dark. I don't need to see that we're a fireball right now.*

Perhaps ten minutes later, everything brightened into a wide view of coastline, city, and ocean. Gravity increased its pull. Second-to-second it grew clearer that they were lying on their backs. The front screens darkened. New images crept up the side screens. Instead of starry black space, Pam stared at endless tan beach with reddish-brown rocks. The engines roared. Spaceport buildings rose up to block the ocean view. One little bump, then the roar cut off. Only the tick and pop of hot things cooling remained.

"Welcome to Solara City. Do *not* release your safety harnesses, yet." The captain explained what was happening, as the shuttle slowly lowered onto its side. Pam's weight shifted from her back to her bottom. "You may *now* unstrap your safety harnesses," she said at last. "Please take a moment to stand, stretch, and get a feel for planetary gravity before you attempt to exit."

Pam and the other candidates wobbled out through the exit corridor to a maze of ramps with railings. *If misery loves company, I guess I have some.* Everyone around her also limped and staggered from the debilitation of hours in abnormally low gravity. Even the Amigos stayed quiet.

She clung to the handrails and lame-leggedly lurched forward. Her aching, rubbery limbs creaked and protested and stretched and strengthened, until she walked *almost* normally by the end of the maze.

Guides from spaceport greeted them. Rehydration came next, then more stretches, then more hydration. *At last!* A rest break in an area with adequate bathroom stalls, adjacent to a room filled with padded chairs and couches. Newscasts glowed on several wall-screens there.

Pam eyed them. *What's happened since I left home?* She lowered her aching body onto a seat against one of the walls and toggled the audio into her implanted Heads Up Display. Plugging in turned the images 3D. *Nice.* Before she'd met Balchu, she'd never paid much attention to news. Now? She smiled to herself. *Guess it's my habit now, too.* Something they still shared, even from far away.

Didn't take long to see Transmondian politics was just as contentious as Ranan politics. Yes, and Transmondian celebrities got into scandals, just like famous Ranans. The wildfires in the Norchellic Republic were bad enough to make Ranan news before she'd left, but now they'd spread. She stared in horror at a clip from the wearable optics of a sheriff's deputy, who struggled to pull a little child from a burning vehicle. *That could be me pulling her out, if I lived there.* She shivered, then sent a wish for safety to her first-responder sisters and brothers in the NR.

Life on a planet seemed needlessly dangerous. Why would anybody choose to live in such an uncontrolled environment? Not that she'd be in danger from the fires here. Solara City lay on the western coast of Monlandia, Chayko's biggest continent. The Norchellic Republic, one of four independent sovereignties on Monlandia, lay thousands of kilometers to the east. But strange dangers loomed everywhere on a planet.

Pam stared at burned-out homes, crowded shelters, and steep, brushy terrain with dense growths of the region's tall, brachiated native life-forms burning like torches. The newscaster called them "trees." True, they filled a similar niche. But how much harder was it to say "ashasatas"? She grimaced. *Okay.* So, "trees."

A weather forecast for Solara City came on. Here was another thing about planets. Pam shifted in her seat. Technically there was "weather" on Rana—soaking fogs at night, with bright, optimal-for-growing light and temperatures between 26° and 32° all day. Here, though . . . sunny today, with a high of 17° and gusting winds, while the low . . . Pam frowned. Seriously? *Five?* That was like being inside a cooler! Could that be right?

A meter away, three women on a couch compared thoughts

about the same forecast, but none met Pam's eye. Did they already know each other? Would it be rude to speak up? Confronting civilian strangers on the job was one thing. But pushing herself uninvited on colleagues? Pam shrank back. *Better not intrude.*

"Up! Up! Time to move!" A groundside staffer swept the area with a stern gaze. All around, candidates groaned and heaved themselves to their feet. Pam's aching, leaden body held her pace to a creaky shuffle.

At least it hadn't been full micrograv for 23 hours! Half-grav was hard enough on a body designed for 1-G. She'd read that Chayko was slightly smaller than Heritage Earth; the gravity here was 0.96-G. Not what she was used to back home, but taxing enough, thanks. She gimped and stumbled through another ramp-maze with the others. Her joints and muscles loosened up faster this time.

Breakfast came next. The buffet offered wondrous variety. Hunger grumbled in her gut, but her first whiff of food brought a queasy backlash. *Ick. Better take this slower.*

She accepted a cup of mild, warm tea and snagged a couple of crackers she found near a soup kettle. Then she settled into a chair with her back against the wall at a narrow table designed for two. No one joined her. Was her face green? She nibbled at a cracker and swallowed hard.

One of the spaceport's uniformed employees approached. "Everything okay?" he asked. "You look a little rocky. How's your stomach? Are you dizzy?"

She grimaced. "I'll be all right."

"Everyone reacts to re-entry differently. Pardon, but you'll need to eat more, before we can release you for the next step in your acclimatization." He aimed a sensor toward her neck, then clipped a pulse oximeter onto her earlobe for a moment. He gave her a packet of nutrients and electrolytes to add to her tea.

Made the tea taste funky, but it eased her nausea. Emboldened, she ate enough to satisfy requirements.

After breakfast more spaceport staffers herded the Ranans through a pair of double doors into a small park. Sweet-smelling plantings of red, orange, and yellow flowers bordered a gravel path. Tall Earth-trees and odd-looking, rough-barked ashasatas offered patches of open shade—not that the shade tempted her. Pam shivered in the chilly breeze.

"Here's another chance to stretch your legs," The staffer by the doors said. "You need to grow better accustomed to the gravity, the light, and such. Stay on the paths. There are benches if you need them, but try to keep moving. The more you move, the sooner you'll acclimatize." A second staffer stood a couple meters down an egress ramp, with a pile of jackets.

Pam gratefully put one on. *That's better!* The jacket bore the XK9 Project's logo of a shield-style badge with a paw print. She moved away from the ramp, then tried a couple of whole-body stretches. *Ugh.* Did several more until they hurt less. No way did she want to feel this bad for four weeks! Or, if a miracle happened, for six months. Those who were Chosen would stay that long.

Chosen. Project literature and her study materials always capitalized the C, like it was some woo-woo mystical thing. And perhaps it was. The OPD'd had to recruit three candidates per dog. The three tiers reflected the recruiters' best estimates of who was most likely to be Chosen, but the choice belonged to the dogs. Dog-directed partner-pairings nearly always remained harmonious and functional, far better than the less-than-50% success rate when humans chose.

Of course, it had been something like seven years since a dog Chose a Third Tier. Better not get her hopes up. Better not think about it at all. Pam bit her lip.

Better to live in the *now.* She let the distractions of this strange, vibrant new world wash over her and clear her worries. An unaccustomed sharp tang teased her nose. Sound filled the air. Creatures whirred or chirped in the depths of the plantings. Leaves rustled and clattered in sharp, gusty palpitations. This was actual wind. It gusted harder than she was used to, a little frightening. Even the most forceful thermals that flowed up the terraced hillsides of Wheel Two's endless, undulating V-shaped valley didn't blow like this. *If only Balchu could be here to see it all!*

Other candidates shared her stretch of path, but no one glanced her way. She spotted the Four Amigos by a railing that overlooked the ocean, their backs to her. They laughed and pointed, clearly delighted by the sound and rhythm of endless waves rolling in. Pam took a few steps toward them. A salty, fishy, wet-rocks smell billowed up. Native creatures with streaky gray coats and long, sharp wings soared above or swooped close. One snapped a breadstick right out of Terry's hand, then powered away with a *scree* that sounded triumphant to Pam.

Patches of shadow and light slid across the park. She looked up at a deep blue sky, dotted with odd clumps of mist. *Clouds.* High fog sometimes gathered near the Station's sky-windows, but these were bigger.

Everything here was bigger. It was all so incredibly *far apart*, and *tall*, and *open!* The orientation lectures had warned that agoraphobia sometimes afflicted Ranans on a planet. Used to a uniform three-kilometer horizon to starboard and port at all times, they sometimes had trouble adjusting. Excitement energized Pam *Ha! No agoraphobia here!*

"Oh, that is so bizarre!" Someone behind her laughed.

She glanced around. A couple meters away two young women in rumpled jumpsuits clung to each other and stared straight up.

"Feels like *we're* moving, not the clouds," the other said.

"I'm dizzy!"

"Yeah, I need to look down for a minute." They laughed again and walked past.

Okay, gotta try that. Pam looked straight up, then staggered. *Woah. Weird sensation!* She blinked, steadied herself with a quick grab onto a nearby bench. *Oh, yeah,* that would've been a lot more fun with a friend to hang onto. Her heart clenched. *If only*

Balchu—she shook her head, chest tight. Balchu wasn't here. Couldn't be. And didn't totally approve of *her* being here.

Get over it, girlie, Mother's voice scoffed from the back of her mind. *Buck up and attend to business.*

The Amigos remained oblivious to her, laughing with each other. They probably wouldn't appreciate an intrusion.

Her throat ached. She walked away down the path. *Here. Now.* She bit her lip and looked up. Beyond the plantings on the far side of the park lay an expanse of angled solar panels. Beyond them rose the fabulous pastel spires of Solara City. Pam's heart lifted. *Oh, wow.*

She'd seen vids, holos, and stills, of course. This was the *real thing.* Some skyscrapers glittered white, some golden, some rose-pink. One sparkled prismatic. Farther away some glowed electric blue, others green, all of them mottled by racing cloud-shadows. They rose impossibly high up into the open air. No sky-windows, just . . . sky. No 25-story height cap, to keep the flight lanes clear for flitters and maintenance crews. *Balchu would love this. It's so exotic!*

Damn. *Did it again.* Unshed tears made her vision swim.

But he truly *would* love this. He would have been fascinated by the shuttle trip. He'd love the ocean, the skyscrapers, the mix of native and Earth-plants. She wished she could send him the chill of the breeze and the smell of the air, the sense of vast expanses. She almost texted him, but then remembered the rate schedule. *Oh, damn. No.* Better snap some pictures and make notes for the diary they were all supposed to keep. She could add it to the free, weekly short-burst letter each candidate was allotted.

She bit her lip and rode out a wave of loneliness, then moved on toward a small grove of aspens. These were Earth trees, like on Rana, not ashasatas. A few steps closer, harsh, raspy, gasping caught her ears.

Pam frowned. Was someone having trouble breathing? She jogged toward the sound.

Seemed to come from that little grove. *Uh-oh. Definitely someone in distress.* Now a man spoke in a low, calm voice. She rounded a clump of tall grass to find her former MUPATS seatmates, the two Beautiful People with Problems.

Ashbea-or-whatever-her-name-was lay on the ground, knees up, shaking and gasping. Her skin had gone whiter than Pam thought possible.

The guy with the micrograv anxiety was on one knee beside her. He looked up at Pam's approach. "Com's dead. Yours?"

Pam tried hers. "Nothing."

"Get paramedics. Run!"

Pam didn't stop to ask. She sprinted back toward the double doors. Several spaceport staffers stood at the ramp's base in a relaxed group.

"Medical emergency!" Pam yelled to them. "Call paramedics!"

By the time she and a staffer with a first aid kit made it back to the grove, the blonde woman lay flat. She looked dead. The guy was administering CPR.

"Anaphylaxis." The guy never paused his CPR. "Epinephrine! *Now!*"

The spaceport staffer fumbled his first-aid kit open.

Too slow! Pam grabbed the rescue injector, popped off the cap, then jabbed it into the woman's thigh. She held it there and counted off the seconds, her heart pounding hard.

The woman gasped, then moaned. "Oh! Oh! Oh!"

"Ashton." The guy stopped CPR, took the woman's hand. "Ashton. It's Charlie. Don't breathe too hard. I know it hurts. Shallow breaths. Steady." He spoke in a calm, friendly voice.

She moaned again. Stared upward blindly with wide, terrified blue eyes.

"We're taking care of you, Ashton." Charlie kept his tone steady, upbeat. "You've had a reaction to something, but you're getting care now. Shallow breaths. That's it. Good."

She blinked, shivered, frowned—but her eyes focused this time. She gave Charlie a confused scowl. "R-reaction?"

"Are you allergic to anything, Ashton?" Charlie's tone remained gentle and calm.

"A-allergic?" Her fitful headshake bespoke her confusion. "No. No, I . . . nothing."

"Don't try to move right now. Just rest."

Sirens approached. Pam leaped up. "I'll guide 'em in."

"Good. Thanks." Charlie kept his gaze on Ashton.

Pam returned to the entrance. Within minutes an ambulance pulled up. "This way!" She guided the paramedics to their patient.

Charlie rapped out a concise, professional-sounding description of the situation, then stepped away to let them work. By now everyone in the park had gathered to watch with worried eyes. The OPD coordinator pulled Charlie and the spaceport staffer aside. Pam started to fade back into the crowd, but Charlie gestured toward her. The coordinator beckoned her over, too.

The Transmondian paramedics took Ashton away.

The OPD coordinator debriefed Pam and Charlie, requested Incident Reports, then turned again to the spaceport staffer.

Pam moved away with a rueful grimace. "Incident Reports."

Charlie's chuckle rolled deep and rich. "Formwork. I sometimes think it's the only language the brass speaks."

She sighed, looked up to meet his eyes. "I think you're right."

He returned her gaze, a little smile on his lips. God, he was gorgeous. A girl could get lost in those big brown eyes. If she didn't already love Balchu . . . .

"I want to thank you." He leaned in slightly, gave an approving nod. "You were rock-solid, instantly. If you hadn't been there, I don't know how I would've managed with no com."

His praise warmed her. How long had it been, since a co-worker said he appreciated what she did? *Too damned long.* She brushed her hair back from her neck, returned his warm smile. "You really seemed to know what you were doing. Are *you* a paramedic?"

His soft laugh held a melancholy note, but little mirth. He glanced down and away. "No, I'm just the driver. Or anyway, I used to be." He shrugged. "Long time ago. Never mind."

Oo, some bitter history there, for sure. "Well, anyway, you were brilliant today. I think Ashton owes you her life. I wonder what she's allergic to."

He looked at her again, shook his head. "Lotta new, strange allergens around here. Native stuff, Earth stuff. No way the screeners could control for all of them."

"They sure *tried*." Pam gave a little shudder. Way too many needle-pricks and check-backs in that process.

His chuckle returned to its original deep-and-rich. "That they did. *Mmm*-mmm, that they did. But she didn't know of any allergies. Probably something Chaykoan." He blew out a breath. "An allergy *that* virulent is bad enough, but our Ashton also just washed out. They'll send her home."

Pam grimaced. "Sucks to be her, then, doesn't it?" She gave him a sidelong glance. "But that makes one less Tier One?"

He was still smiling at her. "Dunno what Tier, but one fewer candidate."

Pleasure bubbled up inside, but then perverse jealousy stabbed. "You seemed to know her. She didn't tell you?"

Charlie shook his head. "We shared a row with you on the shuttle, but I'd never talked to her till we bumped into each other again here."

Sure, that was an accident. Nice but surprising that he'd also remembered Pam was there. She pegged Charlie as a Tier One, himself. Tall, gorgeous, clearly competent, probably whip-smart. No way was he Tier Two material. And definitely not Tier Three. "I don't really know too many of the candidates."

His eyes widened. "Oh! Speaking of which, hello! I'm Charlie Morgan. What's your name?"

She met his gaze with a smile and accepted his handshake. "Pamela Gómez. You can call me Pam."

His brows went up, eyes lively. "Hello, Pam. It's very nice to meet you. Could I buy you a cup of coffee or something? We could get to know each other better."

Pam froze, torn by clashing impulses. "I—I'd love to. But I should tell you I have a boyfriend."

He let out a little sigh. "Back on Rana?"

She nodded.

He gave her a rueful look. "Well, the offer stands anyway. We'll be colleagues for the next few weeks, and maybe longer. Might as well start making friends."

Chapter 3

FATEFUL NIGHT

The Transmondians called it a "campfire." Seemed to Pam it was burning awfully close to the edge of a dense, many-meters-tall ashasata grove. On-Station, an open flame that size would be grounds to call the Fire Department. The wind had died down, but hadn't these people heard what was going on in the Norchellic Republic? Pam gave it a dubious side-eye.

"It was around just such campfires that humans and the wolf-ancestors of today's dogs first met. It's only fitting to for you to meet your new XK9s here," declared Randy, the XK9 Project's Education Director. "This campfire evokes the ancient bond between humans and dogs. Can't you *feel* it?"

Yeah, yeah, whatever. Pam tuned out the rest of his rhapsody on the poetic symmetry of the situation. According to the information she'd studied for one of her exams, humans and proto-wolf-dogs had first met in the humans' garbage pits, when the wolves came in to scavenge food. Granted, a garbage pit would smell worse than Randy's bonfire. Make a less dramatic visual, too.

She shivered inside the fleece-lined jacket she'd been issued. Romantic bullshit aside, wasn't there a nice warm auditorium with padded seats somewhere in Solara City, where they could've done this?

The Project's people had instructed everyone to sit around the campfire. But some damned pebble or twig or something poked her butt, no matter how she squirmed. *Guaranteed* the lovely Ashton would've had another allergy attack out here. It was a miracle more of them hadn't broken out in hives or keeled over.

Plus, it got freaking *cold* here at night. The local weather forecast hadn't begun to prepare her, and the fire's heat did almost nothing to warm her. Roasted on the side nearest the flames, the rest of her remained frozen.

Darkness deepened all around them, despite the firelight. The candidates, the OPD coordinator, Randy the Education Director, and six Trainers from the Project had ridden ten bouncy, rugged kilometers in a pair of buses. All to reach this desolate place outside of Solara City that the Transmondians called a "farm."

Pam cast a disgusted glance across the shadowed premises, which bore utterly no resemblance to Rana Station's sleek industrial farms. Irregular patchworks of stringy, half-dead herbaceous plants sprawled across the open parts. Clearly, these Transmondians couldn't farm their way out of a paper bag.

"And now the moment we've all been waiting for," Randy said. "Let's introduce the XK9s!"

At last! Movement stirred at the edge of the grove, then a man stepped into the firelight leading the most humongous white dog Pam had ever seen. She stared, her heart pounding and her gut like jelly.

Next came a woman leading a black-and-white one that was even *bigger*. Then a russet-colored one, then a yellowish one, then a black one . . . they just kept coming, each dog more ginormous than the last.

Pam couldn't breathe. *Holy shit, Balchu was right.* These things really *were* the size of a damned pony. No XK9 was *ever* going to fit in their apartment. The neighbors would freak out. Hell, *she* was about to freak out. Maybe the firelight and the shadows exaggerated their size?

Well, maybe. *But not damned much.* Good thing she was only a Tier Three!

The giant dogs might come in varied colors, but they all shared that basic wolf-like conformation she'd seen in the illustrations. Furry coat, long brushy tail, large, triangular ears, long legs and muzzle, big teeth. There'd been pictures of XK9s next to humans in the instructional materials, but somehow the colossal size of them just hadn't penetrated.

Till now.

Randy rattled off their names, but Pam was still getting past *my-God-they're-HUGE*. Some had fairly dog-normal names like Scout and Victor and . . . Petunia? Oh, that was the yellow one. Crystal seemed kind of a "well, duh" for the white one. The big all-black one wasn't "Blackie" or "Midnight," though. She missed what they did call it.

One of the dogs had a coat like nothing Pam had ever seen before, light under dark. Kind of hard to see or understand in the firelight and shadows, but interesting. Shady, they called that one. Weird name for a police dog, but not inappropriate for the coat color. Pam kept looking at that one.

"Come on over and say hello." Randy smiled and beckoned, but Pam wasn't the only candidate who hesitated. Others, however, strode right over to the dogs. They held out fists to sniff. Some proceeded to examine the animals' bodies, running hands down legs, lifting lips to examine teeth, even reaching down to check genitalia. Their confident body language made it clear they thought they knew what they were doing.

But Pam could empathize with the lowered ears, the stiff reluctance, the twitches of the fur along some of the dogs' backs. She'd spent a long time studying the "Dog Body Language" materials all candidate-hopefuls had been required to master for one of the qualifying tests. These dogs' body language looked to

Pam as if they didn't like being manhandled any more than she herself would have.

She approached Shady, the odd-colored one.

The tall, burly guy who'd already started examining the animal looked up with a smile. "This is one sweet bitch. Look at that topline, that deep barrel. She'll be a real goer. She'll probably whelp top-notch puppies, too."

Shady laid her ears back. Hackles rose, all along that topline the guy had just praised.

Pam eyed the dog's collar, and the vocalizer mounted there. One of the stranger things she'd learned about XK9s was that they supposedly had a "vocal interface." But no one who'd approached the dogs had so far asked them anything, or spoken to them at all. Curious, Pam said, "Hello, Shady. My name's Pam."

Those expressive, mobile ears went up. The dog lifted her head and gave Pam a penetrating stare that looked almost human.

"You can't be soft around a big dog like this." The burly guy's authoritative tone edged right over into arrogance. "They only respect confidence and strength."

"Hello, Pam." A tinny, somewhat monotone alto voice issued from the dog's vocalizer. "Thank you for speaking directly to me, rather than talking about me in the third person while I am standing right here. I really respect that."

Pam bit her lip, fought a grin.

The burly guy gave Shady a look of outrage. "Here, now! There's no call for that kind of attitude. Sit!"

Ears down, Shady slowly turned her head toward him. She narrowed her eyes, curled her lip to show just a hint of teeth, then lowered her hindquarters smoothly, but not with any great speed.

The guy's face hardened. He almost looked as if he wanted to hit the dog, but he didn't. Instead, he straightened and stepped back. "I . . . think I'll go look at some of the others." He stalked away.

Pam put both hands over her mouth. She struggled to hold in shouts of laughter. That probably wouldn't win her any friends. *But seriously!* That guy had totally deserved it. She looked at Shady.

The big dog watched the guy march off in the firelight. Ears up, mouth wide open, her tongue lolled impossibly long. She'd already regained her feet, and her magnificent brush of a tail wagged high and fast as a fan. She turned to meet Pam's eyes with a look of triumphant humor.

Pam couldn't hold her laughter back after that. She tried to chortle quietly, though. "Oh, God, that was sweet to watch," she gasped, when she could talk again. "I hate it when guys pull shit like that."

Shady cocked her head. "They treat women like that, too?"

Pam sighed. "Some of them do. Not all, thank goodness. But some."

"Unfortunate. I had hoped I guessed wrong." Shady's scary-smart brown eyes studied her. "So, Pam. As you seem to know, I am Shady Jacob-Belle. But all I know about you is 'Pam, from Rana Station.' Do you mind telling me some things about yourself?"

"Sure, if you like. But I'm only a Tier Three." Pam hunched her shoulders. "You'll probably want to partner up with somebody smarter than me."

Shady flicked her ears. "Somebody like Roman Hands, over there? I do not think so. If he is in a higher Tier than you, the Ranans have a strange ranking system. Humor me, if you will."

"Well, okay. What would you like to know?"

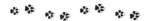

"SHALL I CURL AROUND YOU?" Shady's tinny alto vocalizer-voice asked. "You are shaking very hard. It is painful to watch."

"Your fur does look really warm." Pam huddled in her jacket, unable to control her shivers. The longer she'd stood here, the colder she'd grown. Other candidates had cycled through while she and Shady talked. She probably should've done more circulating herself.

But talking with Shady was like being at a party full of strangers where she'd found someone she really enjoyed. She had a whole month to meet the other dogs, and anyway it probably wouldn't matter because she was only a Tier Three. So she'd stayed with Shady.

"Here. Lean in." The enormous dog's nose nudged Pam close against her furry side, into soft, luxuriant, "black sable" coziness. Earlier in the conversation, Shady had explained that her coat coloration came from a light tan undercoat beneath black "guard hairs."

"This seems a little intimate for a first date, but I'll take it!" Pam snuggled into the offered refuge. *Oh, my.* Shady's side created a blessed field of radiant body heat. That soft, fluffy undercoat wrapped her in warmth. "Your fur is not only fascinating and beautiful—it's *warm!*"

Shady arched her neck and lolled her tongue. "I am happy to share."

"Attention, candidates!" Randy the Education Director called. "I've been told that some of you are experiencing a little difficulty with the temperature." He lifted a hand in the flickering firelight. "Raise your hands, please. Is anyone here in need of a warming station?"

Twenty-eight hands shot into the air. Shouts of "Yes!" "Please!" and "Where can we go?" sounded from all around the campfire.

Randy's face fell. "Oh. Well. Um, in that case let's head back to the bus."

"Thank goodness. I was really starting to worry." Shady's tail waved gently. "I am sorry to say goodbye, but they will not let me go with you."

"It's been such fun to meet you. Thank you for standing in as my temporary warming station." Pam hesitated, reluctant to leave both her warmth and the conversation. The orientation literature had made her expect that talking to an XK9 would be an interface with voice-capable equipment. But Shady talked with Pam like the best girlfriend she'd always imagined but never had.

"Warming you is my pleasure." Shady's big head swung around to press Pam against her side, like a super-sized canine hug.

Pam dared to hug her back. Her throat tightened. "I hate to go. Can't wait to see you again!"

"Me, too. I shall miss you." A soft whimper underscored the vocalizer's words.

They unwrapped from each other.

Yikes! Flash-frozen, much? Pam surprised herself with a quick, impulsive kiss to Shady's forehead, then she sprinted for the bus.

"Pam! Afua! Etsu! Over here!" Cindy, the Trainer assigned to Pam's residence pod, held out a blanket.

Pam accepted it, wrapped up in it, then gave a joyous sigh to discover it had been pre-warmed. "Thank you!"

Cindy smiled. "Pod Three's in Seats K through O. See you there in a minute!"

Pam had been assigned quarters in Dormitory Pod Three, along with four other candidates. She hadn't met any of them before today, although they'd seemed pleasant in passing. There hadn't been much chance to circulate or meet others on the shuttle. Before that . . . Pam frowned.

Frankly, she hadn't wanted to get too close to the others while they were competing for a place on this trip. Promotions were on the line. A new team in the Department, for the first time in most officers' memory. A new avenue for advancement, when it seemed all the advancements were locked in. Some of the other XK9 applicants at lectures and tests had made it clear they intended to make the cut, no matter who they had to sabotage.

At least those were open about it. Who knew how many others were sneakier? Pam had stayed close to the Amigos during the obstacle course in part because she'd felt safer. She always had her guard up, so keeping her distance felt natural. Maybe a lot of the others had felt the same.

She took a seat next to a blanket-swathed podmate named Liz, who'd already huddled close to the heater vent by Seat O. Unlike most of the mass transit in Orangeboro, this bus had been designed with armless seats in five-person semicircles, like a curved, padded bench with shallow depressions for each seat. Pam had learned on the outward-bound trip that the grab-pole in the center of each grouping helped a person slide into place and offered stability on a bouncy road.

She eyed the candidates in other pod-groups, swathed in their pre-warmed blankets. Didn't see any of the cut-throat competitors on this bus. Come to think of it, she hadn't spotted any on the shuttle either. Had the brass screened out the most ruthless? That would be a first. Oh, but there was gorgeous Charlie, sitting near the front with a couple of other guys. He met her eye across the distance and smiled. They hadn't had a chance for coffee today, but maybe tomorrow? She smiled back.

Then Afua, Etsu, and Shuri arrived, all in a bunch. They huddled together for warmth, heedless of seat delineations. *Oh, my.* Pam wasn't the only one who'd been shivering. Without a word, they all closed in on Afua and Etsu, who seemed to be suffering the worst. Pam would swear Etsu's lips had genuinely turned blue.

Cindy had no trouble finding a spot to sit on the end of the curved bench. "I'm really sorry about the cold. Randy's all latched down on that primal campfire thing. At least he didn't roll out the drums this time."

The Ranans exchanged dubious looks. "Drums?" Liz asked.

"Never mind, and consider yourselves lucky." Cindy shook

her head. "We *warned* him Stationers wouldn't be acclimatized for the temperatures. He was actually surprised when some of your group started developing hypothermia symptoms."

Once everyone was aboard, the bus moved out with a lurch and a jounce. It jolted onto a rutted dirt road, then settled into tooth-rattling vibrations.

Cindy smiled at them. "So. What did you think of the dogs? Were they what you expected?"

"Not even a little." Beaded braids swung at Shuri's headshake.

"They're so *enormous*," Liz said. "I really didn't visualize them well, beforehand."

"They're magnificent, I thought," Afua agreed. "So beautiful!"

"And the vocalizers," Etsu said. "That was a big surprise, too. I didn't expect them to really *talk*."

Cindy turned to Pam. "You seemed to hit it off extremely well with Shady. Were you and she *hugging*, at the end?"

Pam hunched her shoulders. "She was trying to keep me warm. It helped."

The others laughed. Pam braced for mocking.

"Oh, wow. Now I'm envious," No mistaking the wistful tone in Etsu's voice. "I bet that fur *was* warm."

"Yeah," Shuri agreed. Each time the bus jolted her beaded braids danced. "I never got that close, but they all looked like walking fur rugs."

The others nodded. Pam couldn't spot a mocking expression among them.

"So, then, which dogs did all of you meet?" Cindy asked. "Who else spent time with Shady?"

Etsu and Shuri had circulated in and out. Pam and Shady had stopped to greet them and several others. Most had arrived in groups of two or three candidates at a time.

The best moments for Pam came between those interruptions, when they could talk one-on-one. She'd eventually told the big dog far more than she normally would've told anyone. About her life as a patrol officer. About Balchu, including his doubts over bringing an XK9 into their miniscule apartment, although telling her that was probably a bad idea. She'd almost said something about Mother at one point, and Pam *never* talked about Mother.

"I kind of circled around between Crystal, Tuxedo, and Elle most of the time," Afua answered Cindy.

"Petunia, Crystal, Shady, and Cinnamon," Shuri said. "Scout a little bit, along with his brother, Victor."

Cindy's eyebrows rose. "Did they tell you they were brothers?"

"I overheard Scout tell one of the other candidates." Shuri shrugged. "Both dogs seemed happy that they're going to Orangeboro together. It appears to be important to them."

Cindy's brow furrowed. "Interesting. I wonder why they attached importance to a relationship like that."

"Tuxedo and Elle said they are mates," Afua put in. "I thought they weren't breeding yet."

"They aren't." Cindy scowled. "Nor are they supposed to 'pair up' like that. I'll have to discuss it with Dr. Ordovich."

Pam bit her lip. Dr. Ordovich was the XK9 Project's head director. Were Tuxedo and Elle in trouble now? Better not mention that Shady said she had a mate too. He was Rex, the huge all-black one. According to Shady, they'd been a bonded pair since they were yearlings. Comparing experiences with Balchu and Rex was a big part of why talking with Shady had seemed so much like talking with the girlfriend she'd always wished she'd had.

"I met Razor, Scout, Victor, and Rex," Liz put in quickly. "I kinda majored on the male dogs, didn't I?" She chuckled. "Didn't even think about that till just now."

The bus stopped, then moved forward on a smoother surface.

"I didn't get much one-on-one time with any of them," Etsu said. "With so many of us there at once, it was hard to get a word in edgewise. But I at least said 'hello' to Petunia, Shady, and Victor."

A pang of guilt stabbed Pam. *Was I greedy to stay with Shady so long?* In the moment, she hadn't really thought about whether others wanted more access.

"Well, I can guarantee you'll get more contact starting tomorrow," Cindy said. "We've got it structured so everyone can meet and do activities with each dog."

Pam resisted the disappointment that wailed through her. Part of her wanted Shady all to herself. The XK9 had an agile mind, an encyclopedic memory, and a wicked sense of humor. She was utterly delightful. But, of course, it was important to meet all of the dogs. Were the others as brilliant as Shady? Pam frowned. Why wouldn't they be? And if so, why wasn't anybody asking whether they were sapient?

Now streetlights strobed past the windows. *We must be back in the city.* Pam craned her neck to look ahead. Soon they drove through the entrance arch at the XK9 Project's main HQ campus. Pod Three awaited inside a dormitory on their left.

Pam stood with the others once the bus halted. She moved forward, muscles stiff and legs kind of itchy after the bumpy ride. Hot chocolate or tea awaited each candidate in the common room of Pod Three. The common room was a comfortable, tan and light-green space with two sofas, a table, and an assortment of chairs. Five single bedrooms opened from it. Pod Three also shared a large bathroom with several enclosed commodes and showers. Hot showers steamed up the locker-room-like space in no time.

Thawed out and swaddled in their blankets, Pam and her podmates emerged a while later for more hot drinks.

Cindy knocked on their door to check on them. "How's it going?"

"Well, I for one am lots warmer now, but there only seems to be one blanket on my bed," Afua said. "Could we turn up the heat?"

"Not unless you want the Project to pass on the energy-use surcharge to the OPD," Cindy said. "Sorry. That's why I brought you each a set of flannel pajamas."

Pam eyed the clothing she'd brought. Their briefings hadn't covered these mysterious Transmondian garments. What function did they serve? "What are 'pajamas'?" she asked.

Cindy laughed. "They're to wear in bed to keep you warm."

Pam and the other Ranans exchanged bewildered looks.

"Who would wear clothing in bed?" Afua asked for all of them.

Cindy's expression went rueful. "This really *is* an unfamiliar climate, isn't it? Pajamas are to keep you warm. How about this: I can issue two more blankets per person, but please *try* the pajamas if you're still cold. Okay?"

"Are you positive we can't just raise the temperature?" Shuri asked.

"Sorry." Cindy shook her head.

Well, damn. Pam gave the pajamas a reluctant second look.

Liz bit her lip. "Um, I have another question, and there's no polite way to ask it." She sighed. "My butt really itches."

"Oh, goodness, mine, too!" Shuri cried. "I was worried I was having some kind of . . . ." She grimaced.

Probably thinking about Ashton. Pam's hot shower seemed to have inflamed several annoying, itchy spots on the lower parts of her body, too.

"Oh, dear." Cindy grimaced. "Anybody else?"

Pam nodded. So did Afua.

"Look." Etsu extended one leg from the folds of her blanket-wrap. Red, irritated-looking spots dotted it from toes to thigh.

Cindy gave her head a dismayed shake. "Xizzes. From sitting on the ground. C'mon. Let's go upstairs to the Infirmary. We'll get you immunized, and there are topical treatments, but I'm afraid they aren't very dignified."

"Anything to stop the itching!" Liz said. "It's on my elbows, too!"

Cindy led their blanket-wrapped parade down the hall. "Some of us warned Randy that you Stationers might not have immunities to things like xizzes. But no. We were gonna have a bonfire, no matter what."

At the infirmary door they met the men from Pod Four, similarly blanket-wrapped. Pam saw a couple of them try to scratch themselves inconspicuously.

Cindy shook her head. "Hypothermia *and* xizzes! Sometimes I just want to smack that man."

Chapter 4

COMMUNICATION AND RESPECT

Pam bade her podmates goodnight, then retreated with her cup of tea to her bedroom, as she had each night all week. She shrugged off the thick "bathrobe" she'd acquired in the Project's commissary on Day Two, then did her nightly stretches.

After that, while she was still warmed up and stretched out and able to reach all the places she needed to, she backed up to her full-length mirror. She pulled a tin with a prescription label from her bathrobe pocket, then applied bright-magenta med-patches to the sites of all her xizz-stings.

They'd scabbed over by now, but both Cindy and the nurse stressed she must continue with the med-patches till the scabs fell off. Cindy's comment that the topical treatments "aren't very dignified" was an understatement. Pam strained to reach, and shifted position for a better view of, her speckled backside.

That's what you get for trying something new. Nothing but a pain in the butt. Mother's voice hadn't risen in her mind as often as usual since her arrival in Transmondia, but she could almost hear her now.

Med-patches *finally* applied, she pulled on her pajamas with a sigh. *Yeah. In this case a literal pain.*

She'd caved and put the pajamas on that very first night. Hadn't dared to go without since. Every day seemed to get colder here. The Transmondians called this time of year "early autumn." They often laughed and added if she thought it was cold now, she'd *love* winter.

Pam pulled the robe on over the pajamas, piled up her pillows, then climbed into bed. She thrust semi-frozen toes deep beneath her three-blankets-plus-a-comforter and grabbed her case pad. Tonight, she must finish her letter, so it could go out to Balchu in the weekly short-burst.

She'd been writing to him each night before bed. Now she glanced back through the diary-like entries, startled to see how much had happened in just one week. There'd been the opening campfire to cap that eventful first day. The days that followed had settled into a routine. Each included work-sessions with the dogs, but the schedule also included much-needed naps and physical workouts to help the Ranans acclimatize. And the schedule also accommodated a surprising number of non-work-related outings.

"There's a time for each thing in your schedule," Cindy had told Pam and her podmates on their second morning. "Too much contact with the dogs, especially at the beginning, can lead to burnout on both sides. These four weeks of candidate-introduction may be the only time some of you get a chance to come to Transmondia. That's why we've tried to organize fun things to do during your mandatory down-time. We'd like to make sure you take at least one half-day or evening for an outing each week."

Sports events included basketball, fútbol, baseball, and a track meet. There were historical tours, scenic tours, trips to assorted museums, an arboretum, a zoological park, and an aquarium. There also were regular group trips to the Solara City Performing Arts Center to take in a concert or other production.

"I joined the Four Amigos for a Maritime Museum tour and a trip to the beach," Pam wrote to Balchu. "It was cold and windy." She'd captured some decent images to send along. Balchu was fascinated by exotic places, and there was nothing remotely like the ocean and the beach on Rana. He already knew about the Four Amigos from Pam's encounter at the obstacle course, so she included snaps of them.

She hadn't included images of Charlie, although she'd mentioned him by name and sketched in the events of the "Ashton incident." She'd snapped a few Charlie-pics, both in the park and during their eventual coffee break. Had a nice one of Charlie smiling at her, but, um, better not give Balchu any needless concerns.

She added views from the inside of the shuttle, the park where the candidates had stretched their legs at the spaceport, the seacoast, and the distant skyscrapers. The bonfire pics hadn't turned out too well. She added one to show him the size of the fire, and another so he could laugh at the Transmondian "farm."

She and her podmates had posed in their pajamas and robes so Cindy could get several group shots with their common room as a backdrop. She sent the one that flattered all of them the most. "I never had girlfriends like this before," she wrote. "We're all so compatible! I guess it takes a certain personality type to be an XK9 candidate. I hope the Choosing at the end of Week Four doesn't ruin our friendships." Liz and Shuri were Second Tier. Afua was First, while Etsu, like Pam, was Third. The law of averages said at least one of them would be Chosen.

She chewed on her lip, then added, "I think most of the candidates are trying not to get too attached to each other, because of the Choosing. I worry about the Four Amigos." She sighed. Surely not all four would be Chosen. But what if one or two were? Where would that leave the others?

A small evasion about Charlie was one thing, but she hadn't been quite honest about Shady, either. She'd mentioned her coat color, her amazing intelligence, and the fun they'd had talking that first night. She hadn't mentioned their instant connection. Hadn't told him she thought about Shady all the time. Nor that she actively looked forward to seeing Shady and caught herself comparing the other XK9s less favorably.

Candidates weren't supposed to pick favorites, but she couldn't help it. She'd also better not mention that there was never enough "together time" with Shady to satisfy her. It would needlessly upset him, and she might get her hopes up if she thought about it too much.

Don't count on anything, Mother's irritated voice snapped from the back of her mind. *Luck don't come for the likes of us.* Yeah, better if she didn't worry him. After all, she was only a Tier Three.

She grimaced, hesitated, then signed off "Love, Pam."

EARLY IN WEEK TWO, Pam, Etsu, Afua, Shuri, and Liz emerged from a RealiCiné production at the Solara City Performing Arts Center, arms linked. Dazzled and exhilarated by an ancient musical drama titled *Les Misérables,* Pam reveled even more in the miracle of real *friends* to experience it with.

Never, *ever* before, had she found girlfriends like these. They'd clasped hands, laughed, and cried through the three-hour epic. They'd muttered their exasperation with the police officer character Javert and the implacable, misguided morality that drove him. The savage ancient system that placed such blatant importance on the value of things over the value of people had, she felt sure, appalled them all. Yes, that attitude was still rampant in much of the Human Diaspora. Mother, for one, never let her forget it.

Didn't mean a person had to accept it as inevitable, though.

They exited into a cool, clear night unlike anything on Rana Station. As one they heaved a collective sigh.

"That. Was," Pam began.

"The. Most epic. Amazing," Afua continued.

"Show I ever saw!" Shuri cried.

Liz laughed. "This calls for—"

"Ice cream!" Etsu shouted.

They dissolved into laughter. *Yes. Ice cream. Totally.*

They were sharing each others' flavor choices using tiny pressed-bamboo spoons, when Pam remembered to turn her HUD back on. A small, blinking alert caught her off-guard. *What? Who? Oh.*

Balchu had sent a reply to her letter. He'd even paid for it, rather than wait for the weekly short-burst. A flutter of mixed joy and alarm shot through her. She focused on her ice cream, but hugged the knowledge of Balchu's letter close to her heart. Mentioning it to the others might break the mood.

So she compared thoughts about the show, laughed, and sang little snatches of half-remembered lyrics with her friends on the ride back to Pod Three.

Only after she and her tea had arrived in her bedroom—only after she'd done her stretches and applied a last few magenta med-patches—only once she'd settled into bed, did she open Balchu's letter.

"I'm more envious than I thought I would be," he wrote. "The things you're seeing and doing sound amazing. I miss you *so much.* I want to be with you *so much!* Every day. Every minute. Way more than I expected, and I already expected to miss you horribly."

Pam paused, torn between her evening's joy and Balchu's anguish. She missed him, too. She'd wished a thousand times already that he could see one or another thing with her. He was more than her lover.

Until this week, he'd been her only real friend. He'd found a way in, past her stubborn, fearful barricades, as no one else ever had. He'd warmed places within her that she'd barely known were frozen. Without his encouragement, would she have been bold enough to try for the XK9 program? Without having known his love, would she have allowed herself to open up enough to find friendship with her podmates? Or with Shady?

She wiped away a tear, blinked until she could see again, then read on.

"I'm going to be honest, here, although I'm worried it'll make you mad," he wrote. "I'm *glad* you'll only be gone for four weeks. I want things back to normal. I'm *glad* you're a Tier Three. I don't even want to *imagine* not seeing you for six months!"

Pam closed her eyes, heartsick. The pit of her stomach radiated toxic cold. *How can we be in such different places on this? How can he still not understand?* With every day that passed she grew more dissatisfied that she was only a Tier Three. More worried that she'd have to face a future when Shady lived on-station, but was partnered with someone else. *Had Chosen someone else.*

Hot tears flowed down her face. *What have I gotten myself into? What was I thinking?*

She couldn't stop herself from crying. The evening's emotions, the changes she was going through, the pain of separation all crashed down on her. After a while, the storm abated. She blew her nose. Took long, slow, calming breaths. Pain closed her throat, clenched her heart. She breathed through that pain, until she could see to read again.

"I went to a Families' Meeting," Balchu's letter continued. "That's a support group the OPD set up for candidates' families. It was all right. They served cake and showed a vid from the XK9 Project, but it was just a promotional vid. You weren't in it. There was nothing about your group or what you're doing. The meeting actually kinda made me miss you even more."

He wrote generalized stuff about the cases he was working. "I wish we could talk. I'd love your insights. God, I miss you so much!"

He didn't say anything about Shady or any of the other dogs she'd mentioned in her first letter. Did that mean he didn't think they were important? Was he in denial, or was she? Her head hurt. Her eyes and her throat and her heart ached.

He'd signed his letter, "Yours always, Balchu."

She stared at those closing words for a moment. Icy tendrils of doubt about "always" sent a shiver through her. His words *I want things back to normal* haunted her. Her old, normal life with Balchu seemed long ago and far away. Was it possible to go back, like this trip never happened? Did she even want to do that?

Pam re-read his letter twice, then closed the file. Her tea had long since gone cold. She left the cup on her nightstand and turned out the light, but it took a long time before she drifted into sleep.

"DAMN IT, PAY ATTENTION," a man's voice snapped. "It's got to be over here."

Pam looked up. That sounded like Mark, the burly fellow who hadn't liked Shady's attitude at the campfire more than a week ago. She scanned the exercise area.

"It is stronger where I indicated." A hint of a growl underscored a baritone vocalizer-voice.

Pam, Liz, and Shuri had been working with Irish-setter-red Cinnamon on this scent-card exercise. Scent-cards were stiff strips about 6 cm. long, with an overlay they peeled back to reveal a sterile surface primed to preserve scents. The candidates had been practicing the proper way to sample a scent, then securely preserve it as evidence, since early in Week One.

"That's Razor's voice." Liz stared across the practice ground with a frown.

There he is. Pam spotted him at last. Razor stood stiffly, ears laid back.

Mark faced him, scowling. "Why would it even be there? That makes no sense."

Pam frowned. Mark was forgetting the number-one rule, "trust your dog." But then, Mark was an asshole.

Razor had classic "police dog" black-and-tan markings, with a tan body, a black saddle, and an all-black face. His alert amber eyes met Mark's gaze with fierce intensity and not the faintest hint of submission. "You cannot smell the target scent. I can. I will not agree to something that is not the case, just because you tell me to." He backed his vocalizer-generated words with a more obvious, deep-chested growl. "That is falsification of evidence, and a crime."

Liz shook her head. "He's really making Razor angry. What is he thinking?"

Shuri glanced toward Liz. "I heard the growl, but Razor looks like he's staying calm enough to me."

"See the tension in his ears? That little flash of teeth?" Liz shook her head. "Oh, man. Mark is trading in dicey goods on thin, thin margins."

Cinnamon's tongue slid out in a loll Pam had come to recognize as laughter at silly humans. "Mark is an idiot and a bully. No one in the Pack respects him. He might as well go home now." She turned to Liz. "You read Razor well. Those are subtle body cues."

Liz kept her concerned gaze on Razor. "Well, thank you, but they didn't seem all that subtle to me. Razor's whole demeanor is keyed up, for him."

Cinnamon wagged her tail. "Razor said you are sharp. I see he was correct."

Liz gave her a big-eyed look. "Razor said that? About *me?*"

Pam swallowed a surge of jealousy. That was the kind of favorable evaluation that might get Liz Chosen.

Cinnamon's tongue-loll was clearly meant for Liz now. "We in the Pack have long since decided which candidates we respect, and which we do not. You are observant. We like that."

Meanwhile, Cindy and Omi, the two Trainers in charge of this session, had called a break. They separated Mark and Razor. Omi escorted Mark out of the activity area, while Cindy spoke in low, earnest tones with Razor.

Shuri sighed. "What'll you bet me they send us back to the pods or change activities entirely, after this?"

Cinnamon cocked her head, then elevated her nose. "What odds will you give me that Mark is being scrubbed from the program right now?"

Pam gasped. "Why do you say that?"

"Omi is furious with him. This is not the first time they have spoken to him about his interactions with Pack members." Cinnamon laid her ears back. "Cindy is right to be worried about Razor's temper, too. He is prancing right on the edge of doing something unwise." She shifted her gaze to Liz. "You should go over to help her calm him."

Liz's eyebrows shot up. "Me?"

Sudden certainty filled Pam. "Yes, *you*. You can help him regain control of himself. You know what to do."

Liz's back straightened. "Actually, you're right. I do." She walked over to Cindy and Razor. Pam couldn't hear what she said, but Cindy smiled and stepped back. Razor's ears went up, his eyes softened, and his entire back end wriggled with pleasure, driven by his enthusiastic tail. Liz's mere presence changed his entire focus and mood.

Tears filled Pam's eyes. Her chest hurt, as if her heart was being squeezed in a vise. Would Shady react to *her* that way, in a similar situation? Or did Shady's devotion belong to some other candidate?

Shuri chuckled. "I guess we know someone Razor might Choose."

Cinnamon lolled her tongue. "You think?"

Cinnamon had called it, regarding Mark's fate. He packed his things and moved out of his pod that afternoon before supper, escorted by Randy, the OPD coordinator, and Project Director Ordovich himself. Despite his bravado at the campfire, he hadn't made it to the end of Week Two.

Pam, Liz, and Shuri exchanged wide-eyed looks when they heard the news, but none of them spoke the next thought. If Cinnamon had known Mark was being terminated, did she also already know whom Razor would Choose?

WHENEVER THE LUCK of random remixing paired Pam with Shady for activities, they invariably settled into comfortable, easy, mutual patterns and rhythms. It was kind of like how it felt to settle into compatible rhythms with her podmates, almost without trying. How could something that had eluded her all her life, suddenly happen so naturally and easily? What magic had changed things?

She dared to ask Shady that question on a scent-trail run, one afternoon during Week Three. Running scent trails with Shady was Pam's favorite activity, because it gave them so many chances to talk without being overheard or interrupted. She'd just finished sampling a scent from beneath a fallen tree and coding the scent-card, when the question popped out.

Shady lolled her tongue at Pam. "It undoubtedly has changed because you have changed."

Pam frowned. "I don't think *I've* changed that much."

"It is the only way such things can happen. Something inside changes, then outward things react." Shady's tail made broad, happy strokes. "I can clearly smell the shifts in your scent factors since that first night we met."

Pam knew better than to ask how well Shady remembered what she'd smelled like that first night. XK9s had been bred to have highly accurate memories, especially when it came to scent. It made their comparisons admissible in court. It also made winning memory-based arguments with them impossible. "Scent factors trump everything else for you XK9s, don't they?" She asked instead.

"Of course they do. You know that." Shady's tongue-loll said she was a silly human to doubt it. Emotion-linked involuntary scent changes reportedly made humans an open book to XK9s. Their unofficial motto seemed to be *scent factors do not lie*.

Had she changed? Well, maybe. "What changed in my scent?" Shady leaned her face against Pam's chest, nose down. Her nose-tip came level with Pam's waist in that position. She seemed to enjoy doing it, because she did it often when they were together but unobserved. "You are more confident now. Still subject to depression, but less closed. You have moved past being afraid so much."

"I wasn't . . . ." Pam grimaced.

"You were. But perhaps you have heard the quote about how the other side of fear is freedom?"

Pam frowned. She absently stroked Shady's neck and gave her ears a meditative scratch. Then she smiled. Maybe that semi-reflexive response was why Shady leaned her face against Pam's chest so often. She chuckled and resumed stroking Shady's neck. "I guess maybe there have been a few changes."

"A few, yes." Shady's tail waved high with amusement.

Pam grinned. "Maybe hanging out with dogs is what changed my attitude."

"If that is true, it pleases me." Shady's nose bumped her, then pushed as if she'd like to bury her whole face in Pam's torso.

Pam staggered back a step. "What's with the full-face press? That tickles."

"I want to fill myself with your personal scent. It is very pleasant."

"Are you saying I smell good?"

"You smell delightful."

Pam laughed. "Just don't knock me over, okay?"

"Hang onto me. I would not let you fall."

Pam bent forward. She leaned her cheek on Shady's fluffy neck.

Her com buzzed. "Are you and Shady lost?" Cindy asked. "Everybody else is back."

Oops. She'd lost track of time. "Coming!"

Chapter 5

UNSETTLING REALIZATIONS

Short-burst night! Pam swallowed a stubborn lump in her throat and strove to ignore her queasy gut. Everyone hurried to clean up after their last exercises with the dogs and dashed through dinner. No one took the night off to go into Solara City. Hard to believe it was the end of Week Three.

Pam had already filed her letter for this week. She'd finished it last night, and nothing that had happened today made her want to change it. On Week Two she'd come clean about how she felt toward Shady. The letter set for short-burst exchange tonight laid it out in the clearest language she could find.

"I'm doing all I can not to think about Choosing Night. It's like an impending doom," she'd written. "Shady will Choose wisely, because Shady is wise, brilliant, and altogether wonderful. But Choosing wisely means *not* Choosing a Third Tier candidate with a one-bedroom walk-up apartment and a housemate who doesn't want an XK9 living there."

Her better judgment told her it was stupid to get attached to Shady, but Pam couldn't find any way to keep herself from feeling what she felt, unwise or not.

Balchu hadn't written back since his early letter during Week Two. Perhaps she'd get a note tonight. Unlike some of the hearty eaters in the refectory, she barely put any food on her plate. Then she couldn't worry down all that she did take.

Shuri and Etsu put their arms around her.

"He'll write tonight," Etsu said.

Shuri nodded. "He will if he's as good a man as you say."

They walked back to Pod Three, still arm-in-arm. No one had to say anything. Pam had never experienced anything like this. All were anxious for their own letters from home, but the acceptance and understanding that surrounded her filled her with amazement. Shady sometimes talked about "pack love" between herself and the other XK9s. Was this how it felt?

Liz, Afua and Cindy arrived a few minutes after Pam's group. They all shared hugs, then everyone sat in the common room holding hands. No one attempted small talk. Pam's anxiety over a hoped-for letter from Balchu balanced oddly with others' eagerness and the sense of oneness in this room.

Then her HUD buzzed. A bright-red dot blinked on her *Incoming Messages* line.

Everyone leaped up.

"Hope it's all good news!" Cindy called to the Ranans.

"Thank you!" Pam answered, but she didn't look back.

Her xizz-stings had long since dried up. The stretches could wait. The tea could wait. She climbed into bed.

"Hi, Pam," Balchu wrote. "Sorry I haven't written in a while. Not sure what to say, especially after your second letter. You're kind of scaring me, talking about Shady. Don't get me wrong. She's probably a great dog, but you know how big our apartment is."

Pam frowned. Read on.

He shifted into generalities about his cases. The kidnapper case had gone cold. They weren't making any progress on the slash distributor. But they'd finally nailed a sapient-trafficker in the Entertainment District. "I was wrapping up for the Borough Attorney," Balchu wrote. "The tip that started the case came from a night-patrol officer, and I checked. It's a guy you mentioned. If you see Charlie Morgan, tell him we got them, and thanks."

Pam laughed, startled. Oh, that would be fun. A gold-plated, *boyfriend-sanctioned* reason to talk with Gorgeous Charlie. She and Charlie had been on different schedule rotations since Week Two. She'd barely seen him at all. Now she had a reason to search him out, perhaps at breakfast. *Some days, you win one.*

"Went to a couple more families meetings," Balchu continued. "They're planning a watch party on Choosing Night. Not sure I'll go. I mostly just stand around at those meetings. No good at small-talk."

Pam stopped reading, heartsick. She knew that odd-man-out feeling. She'd stood around feeling awkward, way too many times. Nibble a cookie, drink a little punch. *Poor Balchu!* He must've been miserable.

"Mom asked if I wanted her to come with," Balchu's letter continued. "She asked if your mother went. Too weird!"

A whole barrel of tangled-up emotions ambushed Pam. She blinked away tears. Dammit, here she was, crying over another one of Balchu's letters. She took several long breaths and reined in her angst. Clearly, Mother and Balchu's mom weren't cut from the same cloth. Punch and cookies and nice, respectable families and . . . and *Mother*?

Oh, hell, no. Balchu was right. That was way too weird.

She sighed. Balchu's mom sounded sweet. *That was a generous offer, especially since she doesn't even know me yet. Maybe I should finally take his parents up on one of their dinner invitations. If we survive this separation, we—*

She gasped. *No! WHEN we survive. WHEN.* She was *not* going to think "if."

❖❖ ❖❖ ❖❖ ❖❖

COFFEE only somewhat dented Pam's headache the next morning. It continued to throb. She dragged herself into the refectory almost late. Most of the other candidates had already finished and left. Her night had yanked her between dreams about breaking up with Balchu and others about Shady Choosing strangers who weren't even Ranans. Dispirited, Pam stared at the donuts, muffins, and scones. Couldn't face eggs or sausage. *Maybe a little yogurt?*

She arrived last of her five-candidate group at the exercise yard where they were supposed to run scent trails with Scout and Elle. Time to put on her game face. She'd worked her beat plenty of times on short sleep. It went with the job. But today she needed to do a lot more than patrol and keep an eye out. She could chat up a shopkeeper or halt a pickpocket at only half-brainpower, but today . . . .

She fumbled numb-fingered for a scent card, then dropped it on the ground. *Stupid. Get with it!* "Sorry." She grimaced, grabbed up the ruined card, then realized she'd contaminated her glove. *Great.*

"Okay, just stop. Please. Stop." Elle's ears clamped flat against her skull as if pained.

Humiliation heated Pam's neck. "Sorry."

"Look at me." She locked onto Pam's gaze with a determined sheepdog-stare. "Stay. Right. Here."

Elle trotted over to Omi the Trainer. "Excuse me, please. I need to take Pam aside and talk with her. It has an impact on this exercise."

Omi's brows rose, but she nodded. "Don't take too long."

Elle turned to Pam. "Come with me." She was about Shady's size, but russet-red like Cinnamon on most of her body, with a bright white ruff, belly, and tail-tip.

Pam followed her up a small hill, out of earshot from the others.

Elle laid her sheepdog-stare on Pam again. "What is wrong?"

Pam blew out a breath. She knew better by now than to lie to an XK9. "I had an upsetting letter from my boyfriend last night, and I didn't get much sleep."

Elle's ears went down again. "This is the boyfriend who thinks your apartment is too small?"

Is nothing a secret from the Pack? "Yes."

"What did he write that upset you?"

Pam's stomach twisted in a knot. "It's family stuff. About my mother. And his mom. And the families' meetings the OPD is hosting, and Choosing Night, and . . ." Her throat closed tighter and tighter until the words squeezed off. *Oh, hell.* Tears streaked down her cheeks.

Elle stepped closer, reared up on her hind legs. Quick tongue-flicks licked away the tears. "That is what I thought. You are in no state to do exercises. You should stand down for the rest of the day." She rubbed her broad head against Pam's side. "I promised Shady I would look out for you. It will be all right."

Pam let out a shuddering breath. "God, I hope you're right."

"Take a moment to regain your composure." Elle stayed right beside her, a sturdy, comforting presence.

Pam stroked her fur, gulped air. Composed herself breath by painful breath. She straightened. "Th-thank you."

"Take your time."

"But Omi—"

"Breathe. Calm. I shall deal with Omi." She trotted away, back down the hill.

Pam followed more slowly. Sleep-deprivation still dragged at her, but breathing came easier. Her nausea subsided.

Omi gave her a frown when she arrived. "Come with me."

So much for breathing easier. Pam followed Omi out of the exercise yard. *Did I just blow my last chance?*

The Trainer walked several meters beyond the gate before she stopped and turned to give Pam a long, evaluating look. "The XK9s on this exercise agree that you are too upset to work. What do you say?"

Pam's stomach did a flipflop. *Could I please just melt into a humiliated puddle now?* "If I was home on patrol, I'd have to work through it."

"Sometimes people try to 'work through it' on the job, but aren't as balanced as they think." Omi's frown deepened. "They can throw a whole team off. *Especially* an XK9 team. The dogs pick up on your energy. They're *dogs*. They reflect us. If we're not right, they're not right. If they're not right, it's *our* fault."

"Are you sending me home?" Pam's gaze flinched away from her. She stared at her feet. "L-like Mark?"

"Oh! No!" She looked up to see Omi's horrified expression. "Please. No. I didn't mean to give that impression at all. You're normally excellent with the dogs. They like you."

Relief made her knees wobbly. "Oh, thank goodness!"

Omi offered a rueful half-smile. "Understand that XK9 field work is different. The dogs *always* know if you're having a bad day."

"'Scent factors do not lie.' Right?"

"Exactly." Omi nodded. "Nor does your body language. Humans give off a thousand subtle 'tells.' Dogs have been studying us for millennia, so they're acutely attuned to our moods. That's a two-edged sword."

Got that right. "Understood. So . . . Now, what?"

"So, you have the rest of the day on stand-down." Omi's mouth was a grim line. "I'd suggest you deal with whatever's throwing you off. The Project has an on-call counseling service, you could choose an activity, or you can stay in your quarters to journal, meditate, or whatever. Your decision."

Pam hesitated to see a psychologist she didn't know. Mother might call the Listeners at home *nosey shrinks* and worse, but they'd helped Pam with some things in the past. It took a while to establish trust, though. Given half an hour's notice and unwilling to sit alone in Pod Three all afternoon, Pam grimaced. "What are my outing options?"

"Well, let's see." Omi pulled out her case pad. On half an hour's notice, Pam could arrive late to a fútbol game between two teams she'd never heard of, or go to the Museum of Ancient and Contemporary Art.

Some choice. She'd already heard tales about the fervor of the fútbol fans in Solara City. Half the attendees would arrive in body paint to match their team colors, half would arrive already drunk, and the yelling could damage one's hearing for life. She didn't know much about ancient or contemporary art, but there probably was no better time to learn than today.

She arrived via taxi alone. Morning- and day-off people already had left. No one else would come from the Project for at least another couple of hours, when afternoon time off officially began.

Museum admission was free. Kinda made up for the taxi. *Kinda.* She wandered from gallery to gallery.

"The World of the Post-Impressionists," she read, at the entrance to one. She went in . . . and there was Charlie.

She stopped. Surveyed the situation.

Charlie stood very still, hands clasped behind his back. He stared at a blotchy painting of a twisted tree, with a rapt expression on his face.

About a meter behind him stood two women. They stared at Charlie with appreciative smiles. Pam didn't recognize them. They must be Transmondians, who'd . . . *what?* Gathered here to enjoy the view? Granted, Transmondian men seemed to run generally a bit shorter, chunkier, and less fit than Charlie. And he *was* easy on the eyes.

But yikes.

Charlie crossed his arms, moved closer to the painting. He bent low and to the left, perhaps to look at the ridges of thickly-applied paint.

One of the women sighed, then sidled closer to him. The other's gaze stayed glued on his glutes.

Dear God. Did their admiration of his backside feed Charlie's ego, or was he irritated by it? Or had he even noticed? Whatever, if she stayed in this gallery much longer, she might be ill.

Mother's voice whispered from the back of her mind. *Rich boys love to play with a girl's heart.* Was Charlie like that? His polished manners and the quality of his civilian clothes told her he must come from one of the Station's well-established Chartered Families. He sure wasn't buying that wardrobe on a patrol officer's pay alone. His Family must have money.

"Sir." That was a museum guard. She stepped closer to Charlie.

He glanced up. "Sorry. I was looking at the way he applied the paint."

"I can't let you breathe on the painting."

"You're right. Sorry. I kinda got lost in it." He stepped back. "I've never seen a genuine, original Van Gogh before. Even the high-rez holograms . . . there's just something about an *original*."

The guard smiled. "It's pretty amazing, isn't it?"

"Yeah." He stared at the painting with something like awe.

Pam backed away quietly and revised her estimation. No ego in play just now, necessarily. He might not have noticed his fan, um, *base*. Whoever this Van Gogh was had riveted the man completely. She glanced at the blotchy tree. *Wow. I guess it takes all tastes.*

She moved on to a different gallery. She was trying to make sense of a Kandinsky a while later, when someone behind her said, "Pam? Is that you?"

She turned to find Charlie smiling at her. She laughed. "I see you managed to tear yourself away from the Temple of Van Gogh."

He sighed. "You know he was a missionary in Belgium for a while? It took him most of his life to figure out his true calling."

She knew no such thing. "Ironic?"

"Yes. Unfortunately, I can relate." He offered a rueful look. "I didn't know you liked art."

She hunched her shoulders. "I kinda got told to take the afternoon off." She gulped in a breath. "By the way, I have a message for you. From my boyfriend."

His brows rose. "The one who thinks your apartment's too small?"

She gaped at him. "Does *everyone* know about that?"

He laughed. "I heard it from Rex."

"Shady's mate, though we can't say that in front of the Project people."

"Apparently not." He shook his head. "Wheels within wheels, eh? So anyway, what's the message?"

"My boyfriend's in the Vice Unit. A while back you gave them a tip." She told what she knew of the trafficking investigation, its happy outcome, and Balchu's appreciation.

Charlie's grin grew progressively through her retelling. He widened his stance, set his hands on his hips and inclined his head toward her. He nodded when she finished. "Oh, that's good to know. Please thank him for telling me. I kept seeing those kids, out at all hours. I *knew* there was more to it than just vagrant juveniles." His smile faded, but his eyes kept their warmth. "We front-line folks usually don't get to hear how it all turned out."

"Too true." She met his eyes, exulted in a moment of electric connection, then flinched away with a guilty pang. "I-I've guarded lots of perimeters with no clue what was happening, other than immediate events. Or non-events, if the lead went bad."

"Mmm, I've done a few of those." His gaze lingered on her face, her lips.

His warm regard roused pleasant tingles in all the right places. Guilt stabbed again, harder. She looked away. Tried to focus on the art, but it was all multicolored clouds with squiggles and lumpy shapes. "What is *up* with this artist?"

Charlie laughed. "You're not a fan? He'd be dismayed. He wanted his artwork to resonate with the viewer's soul."

"Um, sure." She eyed it dubiously. "I guess it resonates. In a jangly sort of way. But I liked your Van Gogh tree better."

His grin broadened. "*That's* in a class by itself. It's also one of the few actual originals in this part of the museum. These are all high-rez holos."

She remembered his exchange with the guard earlier. "Not quite the same experience."

"Somehow, no. Often not." He shrugged. "I take it you like art?"

"I don't know a lot about it. This—" She waved her hand to indicate the Kandinskys "—is kind of mystifying."

He nodded. "It's not for everyone. How about if we stop for lunch, and then I'll show you some things I bet you'll enjoy more."

She hoped he meant *artwork* she'd enjoy more. "I think the museum has a restaurant. It's my turn to buy the coffee."

PAM STOPPED at the exercise area's gate, two mornings before Choosing Night.

"You okay?" Liz joined her, followed by Afua.

"What's wrong with this picture?" Pam asked.

Afua frowned. "Fewer people than usual."

"Same number of Trainers. Fewer candidates." Liz bit her lip.

"I haven't been free to go to Solara City since my art museum trip, but Shuri and Etsu are on their third excursion this week," Pam said.

"I took Monday night off, but that's been it," Afua said.

"And I wasn't offered any time off at all." Liz sighed. "Oh, Pam. I hate to jump to conclusions."

Pam's breath came short and painful. "I know what you mean. But it's been the same dozen-to-fifteen people at all my sessions for the past two days."

"Who have you noticed?" Afua asked. "I keep seeing us, Berwyn, Misha, Charlie, and the Nerd Queens."

Pam nodded. They'd started calling Georgia, Arden, and Connie the Nerd Queens. All three were hardcore physics geniuses from the OPD Bomb Squad.

"Emiko, Mateo, Walt, and Eduardo," Liz said. "And Nicole. Oh. And Russell."

Russell had joined the candidate cadre from the Crime Scene Unit. No surprise he'd earned the nickname Scent-Card Whisperer. Pam nodded. "And us."

"Lot of First Tiers." Liz, from Tier Two, looked worried.

Pam's stomach plunged. If a Second Tier was worried, what were her chances? Except . . . well, she *was* still here. "I talked with Ben, Tim, and Terry at supper yesterday. They've taken up surfing in thermal wetsuits, but said Berwyn's completely gone to the dogs."

Afua laughed. "That sounds like something they'd say. D'you think they have hard feelings?"

"Doesn't seem like it. Far as I can tell, they're all surf-crazy and happy for the extra time to pursue it." There was no surfing on Rana, after all. Pam hoped she was right about the men's lack of jealousy. It would be a shame to break up the Four Amigos.

"We're down to half of the original thirty, if we counted right." Afua's brow puckered. "Does this mean we're the semi-finalists?"

"The Final Fifteen." Liz's worried eyes met Afua's, then Pam's. "Woah. This is getting intense."

"Like maybe we have a real chance." Afua hunched her shoulders. "Oh, wow."

Balchu would have a panic attack if he could hear us. Pam swallowed hard.

Against her better judgment, she did a mental inventory. Afua was a Tier One. So were all three Nerd Queens. Berwyn was, according to the Amigos. Utterly badass Nicole, the Amazon who was stronger than some of the men.

Charlie, almost certainly. She paused her count. *Ah, yes. Charlie.* Then she scowled. *Gotta stop that!* Where she? Charlie made seven, dammit. She'd heard Misha was, too. That made eight of the original ten who'd been recruited. Whether or not she'd guessed right about the unfortunate Ashton also being a Tier One, that meant almost all of the First Tier had made it into Liz's "Final Fifteen."

Afua laughed. "Are you counting the Tiers?"

Pam's gut froze. *Was that rude?* "Yes."

"Okay, so did you get eight Tier Ones? 'Cause that's what I got."

"Yes, I did, if you don't count Russell. Not sure where he placed." She let out a careful breath. "I think I'm the only Tier Three."

Liz grimaced. "They should've moved you up after Mark washed out. He was a Tier Two, for reasons I'll never fathom. You're *way* better-qualified."

She gave her podmate a grateful smile. "Well, thank you." *Makes one with that opinion, anyway.* "Of course, it's all just clueless humans guessing, at this point. Doesn't matter what we think. What matters is what the dogs think."

Speaking of whom, here they came.

Chapter 6

THE CHOOSING

The XK9 Project issued snug, warm boots, thermal underwear, caps, scarves, gloves, and long, puffy, insulated coats for Choosing Night. Pam pulled hers on eagerly. It was colder than holy fucking snowballs out there.

The candidate group was down to 28 members, now that they'd lost allergic Ashton and arrogant Mark. They boarded well-warmed buses by pod-group and returned to the "farm."

Afua and Liz sat on either side of Pam. Without even saying anything, the three linked gloved hands.

"I wonder if there'll be drums this time." The blower on the heaters almost drowned Afua's voice.

Liz grimaced. "I wonder if the inoculations against the xizzes are still effective."

Pam wondered if she'd be able to keep her supper down. She couldn't think of anything clever to add. She drew in a shaky breath.

Her friends' hands on either side squeezed hers. They rode on in silence.

The campfire was bigger this time. There were folding chairs, thank goodness. On the near side stood a little knot of officials, also hatted, coated, and gloved against the icy air. Pam thought she recognized Chief Klein and Project Director Ordovich among them, but they were so bundled-up it was hard to be sure. There also were what looked like several journalists, with little flocks of cameras buzzing overhead.

Randy led the candidates to a section of chairs near a low dais. Cindy, Omi, and the other Trainers retreated into the grove, probably to connect with the Pack. Everyone sat, except Randy. He joined the little knot of officials.

Pam looked around. No drums anywhere. *Good.* Maybe they could get this over with before her toes turned blue. Anyway, frozen drums probably wouldn't sound too good. Randy was probably pissed off that this cold snap had messed up his theatrics.

This time he had a mic. From the sound of things, they'd rigged speakers on the tall ashasatas, although it was too dark to see clearly. Randy gave his spiel about the primal setting and the ancient bond between humans and dogs.

The campfire popped and snapped, but its warmth didn't radiate far enough to touch Pam.

She hadn't been able to take decent images at the first campfire. She also had dealt with enough optical equipment at nighttime accident scenes to imagine what the journalists and camera operators thought of Randy's campfire. Randy maundered on for a while, but finally wrapped up his remarks.

Pam closed her eyes. *Oh, God.* This was it . . . *but no.* Now Dr. Ordovich was talking. It was like being yanked back from the jaws of fate. She sighed. No, more like being dangled just above them, then tortured indefinitely with platitudes. While slowly freezing to death. She balled her hands inside the palms of her gloves to keep her fingers a little warmer, but there was nothing she could do for her toes. She stared into the fire and tried to live timelessly in the *now.*

Ordovich droned on about what a great day this was for both Orangeboro and the XK9 Project . . . largest group yet sold to a police department . . . historic sale . . . incalculable value . . . okay! At last he seemed to be wrapping it up.

"Chief Klein, would you care to say anything?" Randy's voice asked.

Pam wasn't sure how much more of this she could . . . *no. Timelessly in the now, dammit.* She'd heard somewhere that when you were freezing to death you began by feeling warm, and then fell asleep. *Rats. Still cold.* Must mean she only *thought* she was freezing to death. Or maybe it was a superstition. Because she was fucking *freezing.*

"Thank you," Chief Klein said. "I have many thoughts, but primary among them is the desire to avoid exposing my officers to frostbite. Shall we begin the Choosing now, please?"

Pam wasn't sure whether she loved her Chief or hated him in that moment. Her heart rate tripled with terror, but her toes and her fingers argued for "love."

"Let the Pack advance," Randy said.

Here they came. On leashes, again, as if they needed leashes. Leading them out at the first campfire had been theatrics for the candidates' benefit. Now it was bullshit theatrics for the cameras. The Trainers, acting as their "handlers," lined them up between the candidates and the campfire. Every XK9's tongue immediately lolled in a pant—not all of it from nervousness, Pam was sure. They were close enough to the fire to somewhat feel it. The "handlers" removed the leashes, told them to *stay*, and departed.

"Tier One candidates please rise," Randy said.

About a third of the candidates stood. Ha! Who called it? Charlie, Georgia, Connie, Arden, Nicole . . . she'd known for sure that Berwyn and Afua were Tier One, but she'd mostly been guessing about Misha and . . . wow, Russell, too?

"XK9s, Choose your partners," Randy said.

Six XK9s sprinted forward. No hesitation. Rex leaped ahead by a nose. He ran straight to Charlie. *Oh, yeah, that was a match.*

Charlie shouted with joy. Rex play-bowed and wriggled. Pam almost laughed.

Cinnamon ran to Berwyn. The three remaining Amigos whooped and cheered and high-fived. They converged on the new partners for one massive, joyous group hug.

Tuxedo ran to Georgia, Crystal to Connie, Elle to Misha, Scout to Nicole.

Pam and Liz turned to Afua, reached out to her. She sat down slowly, trembling a little. Pam and Liz hugged her. "Which one did you want?" Liz asked, still hugging hard.

"I didn't know," Afua said softly. "I liked several." She blinked, hugged Pam and Liz back with one arm each. It's okay. I'm okay. Look how happy they are!"

And truly, they were. Georgia had her arms around Tuxedo, her face buried in his fur. Misha cradled Elle in his arms, speaking earnest words, his face a study in loving delight. Nicole and Scout matched each other leap for leap, with each leap higher, *higher*, catching more and more ecstatic air.

Cindy, Omi and another Trainer eventually corralled the new partner-pairs enough to guide them into an adjacent field, where they whooped and barked and danced and leaped and hugged and shared their joy.

Pam realized that many of the candidates were clapping, cheering, whistling. So were the officials. So were the journalists. How could anyone resist such open, unbridled delight? This was a *now* it was good to live in.

But eventually the applause faded. The tension mounted once more.

"Tier Two candidates, please rise!" Randy's voice on the loudspeakers ordered.

Liz gasped.

"You've got this," Afua cried.

Liz stood. So did Walt, Eduardo, Shuri, Tim, Mateo and the others.

Pam drew in a shaky breath, then blew it out as a cleanser.

Shady hadn't Chosen a Tier One, although she deserved one. Whom would she Choose?

"XK9s, Choose your partners!" Randy said.

Razor ran straight to Liz, wriggling and squeaking. She shouted with joy, then hugged and hugged him.

Petunia Chose Walt, while Victor leaped to Eduardo. They shouted and danced and yelped and leaped and barked and cried their delight. Two more Trainers rounded them up, then guided them away.

The unChosen candidates rushed toward each other, filling the vacant spaces, together in solidarity. But no one seemed devastated. No one seemed crushed. Everyone seemed giddy. They laughed and chattered.

Then caught themselves, and . . . .

Lapsed into silence, and . . . stared.

As the realization dawned that one XK9 still had not made her Choice.

Everyone slowly sat down again.

Pam couldn't breathe. Everything around her faded away. Everything but Shady.

Shady still stood by the campfire, panting freely. Her eyes locked on Pam. Her tail wagged a slow metronome beat.

"Wow. This is unusual, ladies and gentlemen," Randy's loudspeaker voice boomed. "This is the first time in seven years, but okay! Tier Three candidates, please rise!"

Pam staggered to her feet, only vaguely aware of the others who rose with her. This couldn't be real. She dragged in a breath.

"XK9 Shady, Choose your partner!"

Shady ran straight to Pam.

To her!

There were no words. The whole world went liquid. She fell to her knees.

She clung to that gorgeous black-sable coat and wept.

IT TOOK a while for the Trainers to get all of the new partner-pairs rounded up, herded to the road, and loaded onto a bus. No one seemed bothered by the cold, now. Nobody was in the mood to follow orderly directions. The hugs, the laughter, the joyous barking and running and jumping took a long time to subside. But at last they somehow all had been gathered inside the bus.

The bus's doors closed.

"It's so we won't escape and go dancing off across the fields again," Pam said softly to Shady. "Although I've got to say I'm about danced out." Gradually, the chatter and laughter subsided all around them. It was a pretty good bet that everyone was about danced out.

Shady leaned against her, thumped her tail. "I could rest." She filled Pam's lap with her head. "What a relief!"

"That it's over?" Pam asked.

"That I found you, and went to you, and you did not run away."

Pam shook her head. "Are you kidding? That was the single most amazing thing that's ever happened to me."

"But, your boyfriend. Your tiny apartment." Shady gave her a worried look.

Pam sighed. "We'll work something out." The cold heaviness in her gut argued otherwise. "Or . . . or, we won't."

We . . . hard even to think it, but *we actually might not.* She and Balchu had felt so *right,* from the very beginning.

But she and Shady *also* had instantly connected. Shady had waited all that time for Third Tier. For *her.*

She shivered.

"Shall I curl around you now?" Shady asked.

Pam bowed her head. "It's an inside chill. I am worried."

"I know. That is clear to smell, and scent factors do not lie. How can I help?"

"Don't leave me."

"I am your partner. Why ever would I leave you?"

Pam's view of the world was swimming again. "People do,

that's all. People do." *People had. Balchu might. It happened.* She wiped her face and wished for a tissue.

The bus door opened. Randy and Chief Klein stepped inside, as if blown on a gust of cold wind. They closed the door behind themselves.

"Congratulations, new partner-pairs!" Randy shouted.

A chorus of barks and cheers and applause greeted him, but quickly died away.

"Are you *excited?*" Randy shouted.

Oh, God. Not a pep rally. Pam grimaced.

Klein tapped Randy on the shoulder. "Maybe later. They're exhausted. Tell them what they need to know."

Randy appeared to deflate a little. He shot a glance at the Chief, then eyed the bus's occupants. "Okay. What you need to know about tonight is that we'll be moving you to new quarters. Partnered pairs will live together in their own, specially-designed units, in a different part of the HQ campus. OPD officers, we were advised that you'd prefer to pack up your own belongings and say goodbye to your podmates before they leave for the Station."

Pam smiled. "Thank goodness!" She wanted to stay in touch with Afua, Shuri, and Etsu. They'd shared too many things this month to never see each other again.

"XK9s, you'll meet in the Unpartnered Kennels one last time for chow, then we'll take you to your new quarters," Randy continued.

Shady lolled her tongue. "I definitely could eat."

Randy turned to Chief Klein. "I believe your chief has one more announcement."

Klein smiled. "Before that, I just want to say to my human officers, *well done.* And to our new XK9 officers, welcome to the Orangeboro Police Department!"

Pam cheered and applauded along with the others. Shady and her Packmates barked.

Klein gave a little nod. "Now, the announcement. At my

urging, the Borough Council has granted each of you a spacelink call home tonight, for up to five minutes."

Wow! Pam stared at the Chief. What an extraordinary gift! She added her share of the cheers, whistles, and applause for this. A five-minute spacelink call would cost half a week's pay. The Council's generosity amazed her. She didn't want to know how Klein had finagled that perk.

Klein smiled at them, saluted, then departed.

Chapter 7

A NEW REALITY

Once back at Project HQ, Pam hugged her podmates, exchanged contact information, then hastily packed. She hauled her heavy duffel to the front door. The bus to the spaceport arrived. She helped her friends load their duffels.

Then she shouted, "Good luck!" and "Safe travels!" and waved and waved, until Afua, Shuri, and Etsu were gone. Off to catch a redeye to Rana Station.

"This is really happening," Liz said.

Pam gulped. Her insides went jelly-wobbly. "It really is."

Their new quarters turned out to be six tiny duplex cottages, arranged in a circle. The OPD group took up five of them. Pam and Liz shared a duplex. They'd barely started to unpack before Shady and Razor arrived, eager to sniff every crevice of their new place.

Liz stepped aside for Razor. She turned to Pam. "I'm gonna say goodnight, now. Got a call to make—and, seriously, Pam. *Good luck* with yours!" She followed Razor inside and closed the door.

Pam stood for a moment or two in the quiet. Her heart constricted in a tight, painful squeeze.

Shady detailed their new digs, ears and tail up. So excited! This would be her first home shared with a human partner. Pam tried to give herself entirely to this pleasant moment, but the call to Balchu loomed like a specter in the shadows. *Did he and his mom go to the watch party? Oh, please let me not have to break it to him.* She rubbed her face, took a cleansing breath. Took several more.

A cold wet nose poked her elbow. She looked into Shady's wise brown eyes. "Delaying will just make you dread it more."

Pam sighed. "You're right." She dug out her case pad and parked it on the tiny table. She sat in the unit's single, straight-backed chair, then took a long, slow breath. It was like standing at the edge of a primary terrace back on Rana, teetering on the brink of a hundred-meter plunge.

She put the call through. Held her breath.

It took a subjective *forever* for Balchu to pick up. "Pam! *A spacelink?*" Fumbling thumps, then an image of him lit her case pad.

She'd directed the call to the pad, not her HUD, so Shady could see and hear it, too. Dark, tired rings circled his bloodshot eyes. His hair was rumpled every which-way. He looked as if she'd waked him. "You okay?" she asked.

He blinked at her through the case pad, brow puckered. Unless she missed her guess, he'd gone well past his usual limit of one whiskey after dinner. "So. I guess it's over." He grimaced. "How'd it go?"

Oh, God. He hadn't gone to the watch party. "It, um, went pretty well," Pam said.

He breathed out a cautious sigh. "So . . . you're coming home?"

A frisson of chill zinged through her. "Ye-e-e-es. In an-another five months." She looked toward Shady, who snuggled in close, then stared at the case pad.

"Hello, Balchu. My name is Shady."

His eyes went wide with dismay. "Oh, holy fuck." He stared

into the camera on his end with a desperate, horrified expression. "Pam! Don't joke like that!"

Pam scowled. Did he have to seem *that* appalled? "This is no damned joke, Balchu! We *knew* there was a chance I'd be Chosen! I *told* you how well I got along with Shady!"

"No-no-no-no-no-no-no!" Balchu cried. "Pam! You're a Third Tier! How could this *happen*?"

Shady laid her ears back. "This happened very simply, Balchu. I liked Pam best, so I waited for her group to be called." She added a soft growl. "Do you not believe that Pam is wonderful and worth waiting for?"

"No, that's not the point!" Balchu cried. "Yes—I mean, yes, Pam is wonderful. But—but this wasn't supposed to—*Pam!* Don't do this!"

Pam shook her head, mind spinning. The two realities in her life pulled her opposite ways, like a prisoner on a rack. "I made a commitment, Balchu. I signed a contract. *You* made a commitment too, damn it! You can make your own choice, but *I'm* not backing out."

"But—" Balchu's despairing look reached out through the case pad to clutch at her from the far, far distance. "Oh, Pam. We can't—we don't—" He shook his head. "Damn it, Pam! Where does that leave . . . leave *us*?"

Why must she choose? Why was he doing this *now*? She released a shaky breath, her stomach a cold, hard stone. "I don't know, my love. Maybe it leaves us . . . nowhere at all."

Pain clenched its talons. She ended the call.

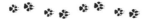

PAM WOKE GUMMY-EYED AND HOLLOW, but not alone. And definitely not cold.

Shady's shaggy fur had kept her warm as toast, even without pajamas. She yawned, blinked, and accessed her HUD's chronometer. Oh! She'd be toast of a different sort if she didn't get moving.

"Good morning. Do you feel better?" Shady commenced sniffing her over in detail.

Pam diverted her new partner's nose from several ticklish places. "Not human, yet. Need a shower."

Shady lolled her tongue. "Oh, you definitely smell human."

"*Mmm-mm.* Too early." She stumbled to the tiny—*private, yes!*—shower, then cranked it as hot as she could stand it. In the back of her mind, Mother's voice snapped at her. *Buck up, girlie. Men come, and they go. Who needs 'em?*

Pam sagged in the almost-scalding water, frozen inside. Other than Shady and her podmates, Balchu had been the most decent, wonderful thing that had ever happened to her. *Why* had he made her choose, when there was no other choice left to make?

All men are idiots. Can't count on a damn one, Mother's voice inside her head mocked. *Get over it. You're better off traveling light.*

She toweled her hair dry and pulled on fresh clothes, heavy with despair. *No lightness here, Mother.* No lightness, but things to do. People to face. *What can I say to them?*

"You will feel better once our Pack surrounds you," Shady said. "Pack is love. There are more of us, now, but that truth remains. Pack is always love."

She shrank from facing anyone. "How can I go out there and act normal?"

"No one expects you to act normal," Shady said. "You have received a terrible blow at a moment that should have been nothing but joyful."

She closed her eyes. Buried her face in Shady's shaggy ruff. "They know?"

Shady rubbed her head against Pam's side. "When we are troubled, we go to our Pack. We share our concerns. The Pack is our family, our heart, our home. After you fell asleep last night, I went to the Pack with my worry. I was very, very upset, but they comforted me. You are now Pack. Let them comfort you, too."

"But I'm a human."

Shady lolled her tongue. "We love you anyway. Our Pack now includes lots of humans."

What a load of sentimental claptrap, Mother's voice mocked.

The ache in Pam's heart intensified.

No surprise, everybody else was already at the refectory. They looked up when she and Shady arrived.

"Pam!" Liz hurried over. She pulled her straight into a hug. Pam hugged back, wordless. Tears leaked without a sound. Shady and Razor circled around. Shady reared up to lick away her tears the same way Elle had. Pam groaned. *What a hot mess I am!* Eventually, she and Liz stepped away from each other.

Liz's worried eyes studied her. "Are you gonna be okay?"

Pam bit her lip, not sure.

Berwyn and Cinnamon moved in. "Oh, girl, I'm so sorry," Berwyn said. "What a terrible thing!"

Liz and Berwyn wrapped her in more hugs. Razor, Cinnamon, and Shady circled around them, panting and pacing. Others drew closer. Hands reached out. Faces filled with concern. XK9 bodies angled and circled, anxious.

Stunned, Pam accepted their hugs and their earnest, unexpected worry on her behalf.

Not a single one of her new colleagues mocked her. Not a single dog or human seemed to think she was stupid to be upset. All they offered was compassion.

Pam could scarcely believe it. "You—all of you—you've known me for less than a month. How can you care?"

"Because you are Pack," Shady said.

Liz squeezed her hand. "The dogs have been very clear about this, and I agree. We're all Pack now. Pack is a kind of family."

"Come over here and sit with us." Berwyn said. "Would you like eggs? Pancakes?"

"Care for some coffee, Pam?" There was gorgeous Charlie,

over by the coffeepot. The caring warmth in his face made her heart skip a beat.

"Thank you." She smiled in anguished gratitude. *Rich boys are great for a short fling, but never count on 'em,* Mother's inner voice snapped. *Don't be an idiot.*

A split-second flash of fury seized her. Pam breathed through it, then lifted her head. *Shut up, Mother.* She smiled and accepted the coffee from Charlie. He'd fixed it just the way she liked.

Next came eggs and pancakes from Berwyn.

Liz's embrace enfolded her.

Shady, Razor, Cinnamon, and Rex pressed closer.

You are Pack, Shady'd said.

Pack is a kind of family, Liz had said.

The acceptance that surrounded her filled her with awe. This was no illusion, no tricky glamour. This was a real, true thing. Pam drew in a deep, amazed breath. *So. This is how it feels.*

- The End -

IF YOU ENJOYED "THE OTHER SIDE OF FEAR" . . .

If you enjoyed *The Other Side of Fear*, please take a moment to **leave a review!** It's one of the very best ways to help an author whose work you enjoy. The **bookseller from whom you bought this book** (such as Amazon or Barnes and Noble) has a form you can use for reviews. Another good place to leave a review is Goodreads.

WHAT HAPPENS NEXT?

The events of *The Other Side of Fear* take place before the events of the XK9 "Bones" Trilogy. *What's Bred in the Bone* (Book 1) comes next in chronological order.

If you haven't yet read it, Chapter One is just a page-turn away. I hope you'll enjoy it!

Look for Book Two of the trilogy, *A Bone to Pick*, in the fall of 2020.

Book Three, *Bone of Contention* is currently scheduled for publication in 2021.

WHAT'S BRED IN THE BONE, CHAPTER 1

By Jan S. Gephardt
A Walk in the Park

Damn it, no horizon should bend upward. XK9 Rex Dieter-Nell flinched away from the "scenic overlook." He clenched his jaws on a quiet whimper, but the shudder down his back made his hackles prickle.

His human partner, Charlie, met Rex's eyes. *I'm sorry. I know you don't like it.* His words flowed through their brain link on a wave of empathy.

Rex lowered his head, wary of insulting his partner's beloved home. Maybe if he switched to using his collar-mounted vocalizer he could achieve more emotional distance. "I think perhaps the taste must be acquired."

But is it one you'll ever acquire? Charlie's worry echoed through the link.

Rex looked away. He shared his partner's concern, but feared to admit it. "It is getting dark. Perhaps we should move on."

Charlie straightened, stepped away from the guardrail. *I know everything's different for you here. It'll take time. Things'll grow less strange. I'm just being impatient.*

Rex'd hoped to spare his partner's feelings, but the brain link had betrayed him again. *I guess we'll see how things work out.* He hazarded another look. *Ugh.* It was freaky-unnatural for a river to run down the wall at one end of the vista, as Wheel Two's Sirius River did. Even worse for it to run back *up* the wall at the other. But this weird quirk of Rana Habitat Space Station's toroidal wheel-geography, in itself, was minor compared to all that Rex had lost.

I appreciate your respect for my feelings about my home. Charlie'd followed his thoughts again. He ran a strong brown hand along Rex's neck, then rubbed the base of his ears with soothing strokes.

Rex leaned into his partner's hand, despite his mood. That did feel pretty good. A soft little whimper escaped. He pressed his head against Charlie's sternum and gave in to the ear-rub.

I don't want to belittle your loss. Charlie's fingers kept up their soothing rhythm. *I know how much you miss your Packmates, especially Shady.*

Rex, his mate Shady, and their Packmates, the ten members of the Orangeboro Pack, had spent every day together at their planet-based former home in Solara City. Together for training. Together for meals. Together each night, nestled in the straw bedding on the hard floor in the Unpartnered Kennels. Together was how they'd always hoped to stay. The Pack, together, meant home, meant family. Meant love.

Rex rubbed his head against Charlie, soothed by his partner's empathy and his comforting personal scent. But a burning knot of longing expanded within him whenever he thought about Shady or his Packmates.

None of the Pack had seen each other since the Presentation Ceremony in Orangeboro's Central Plaza. Each XK9 lived at his or her human partner's home now. Rex and Shady spoke secretly on their coms each night, but that was their only contact. It had been almost two entire months. Charlie'd lodged several protests about the Orangeboro Police Department's policy of keeping the dogs apart. Shady said her partner Pam had too. No luck. The XK9 Project had prescribed these handling protocols. The OPD wouldn't budge. The Pack stayed apart, ten lonely exiles in a bizarre foreign place, with only humans around them.

A howl swelled from Rex's heart, but he swallowed it unsung. Time to change the subject. *At least we did well today. Even if no one else knows.*

Charlie stroked Rex's neck. *We scored a nice win today, and trust me, the right people know.*

I guess. Rex flicked his ears, still dissatisfied. Their subject had been an acrobatic burglar who liked to climb up the local residence towers' outer balconies to gain entrance. Rex hadn't needed to climb balconies to chase her, thank goodness. He'd crossed her trail outside a pub she was known to frequent, then tracked her to a storage unit where they'd caught her literally hip-deep in stolen goods. That had been fun.

But then came the rest of the day. They'd spent it in Precinct Nine Station's Evidence Submission Room. That had not been fun. Rex had helped as much as he could with the inventory. But mostly it was Charlie who'd imaged, ID-tagged, bagged, and deposited everything they'd recovered. Meanwhile, upstairs, DPO Sanchez, the lead detective, received all the congratulations.

Irritation prickled like an itch he couldn't reach. Rex smelled the hot, achey inflammation that lingered in his partner's neck, back, and especially his weaker left arm, although Charlie had not complained. *DPO Sanchez did nothing but tell us a couple of places we might start and hand us a glove for me to sniff. We took it from there. We followed the scent. We solved the case. It was our victory.*

Charlie shook his head. *You know Sanchez has been on that case for months. The glove was crucial, and so was the tip about the pub. Gotta give her that, at least. She deserves the glory.*

Hurt and frustration squeezed Rex's throat. *But I deserve glory, too. Captain Argus had to order her to use us.* He stifled a growl. *Sanchez called me the Chief's new toy. I am not a toy. And you proved it today.* Charlie scratched behind Rex's ears again. *Do solid work, then don't be obnoxious about it afterward. That's the best way to convince a doubter like Sanchez. And as I said, the right people know what you did. Captain Argus and Chief Klein are both very pleased.*

Rex sighed. He was acting like a puppy, longing for praise. At the mature age of seven, he was old enough to know better. Dogs mustn't snatch admiration away from humans. He did know better. But he loved being at the center of admiration. Having a mature attitude sucked.

They turned away from the overlook, headed up the path toward the steps of the next switchback. All manner of scents flowed down from plants, small creatures, buildings, and humans up-slope: residual odors of what people had eaten or scent factors that revealed their moods. Rex recognized several human scent-profiles from past encounters, but the nearest was Charlie's neighbor Fatima Smythe. Rex'd met her at a neighborhood picnic the week he'd arrived on-Station.

Associated with Fatima's location, other new scents filtered down. Ozzirikkians had a characteristic sweet-organic, almost smoky odor, in contrast to most humans' base-scent, which lay in the musky, mellower mid-ranges. They were Rana Stationers, just like humans, but the higher gravity of human habitat wheels made it unusual for them to visit. *What are two ozzirikkians doing here?*

Charlie gave him a sidelong glance. *Ozzirikkians?*

They're with Fatima and one other human, approaching on the path above us. Rex gazed up the path, but the bushes obscured his view.

The link conveyed Charlie's puzzlement. *To venture into our gravity, these ozzirikkians must be close friends.* Anything higher than 0.823-Terran G taxed ozzirikkian joints and organs if they stayed more than a few hours. Charlie frowned up the path, but then through the link Rex felt his realization dawn. *Oh. I bet they're co-workers, here for the betrothal rehearsal. I wonder if they're part of her betrothal party.*

Whatever they were doing here, they drew nearer. Rex caught scents similar to those that humans or dogs emitted when in mild-to-moderate pain. Ozzirikkians didn't come into human territory lightly. They had their own habitat wheels, Numbers Five and Six. Those Wheels were a different size, and counter-rotated at a slightly different velocity from the human Wheels, to provide the proper gravity.

Rex froze, nose high. Here was another new scent, an unmistakable combination of human sweat with scent factors spawned by anxiety, hyper-alertness, and ill-intent. There was nothing else in all the scent-spectra quite like the smell of a human preparing to do something bad. And this human was closing in on Fatima and her friends.

A shrill cry cut the air. No mistaking the person's fear.

Rex sprang up the path. He ran into a cloud of malevolent, aggressive male human scent. Mingled with it, Rex caught the human women's and ozzirikkians' scents, sharp with terror.

"Damned click-apes!" the man cried. "What're you doing here?"

Protective fury swept through Rex. He rounded the bend, hackles stiff and teeth bared.

A slender man in dark clothing confronted Fatima and her friends. He leveled an EStee at them.

Rex cranked his vocalizer to top volume. "Police! Halt! Drop your weapon!"

The man swung around. He fired the EStee in Rex's direction, then plunged into the thicket next to the path. With a crackle of dry leaves, he disappeared.

Rex bounded past the human-ozzirikkian group, focused on

their assailant. He shoved his head and burly shoulders into the brush. Stiff branches tore at him, but he pushed forward by main force. Being larger than any normal dog had both advantages and drawbacks.

The skinny-hipped subject scrambled through natural tunnels under the bushes. Rex's equipment panniers caught in the stiff twigs.

Rex retreated, shook himself, then stepped back to get a better overview. *My panniers are too wide!*

Charlie reached him in seconds. His hands loosened buckles, released hook-and-loop straps. The panniers lifted off. "Can you get him?"

"Consider him got!" Rex lunged into the brush, the subject's scent hot in his nose. The tunnel twisted. Rex rammed his way through the tough branches.

His quarry's scent went sweaty-cold with terror.

Good. Rex's growl thundered in his chest. He shoved through the bushes.

At the edge of his attention, he sensed Charlie. His partner strove to calm the victims, called for backup. Charlie was covering his end of things. Rex had a different mission.

Rex's quarry doubled back, dodged, evaded. Always stayed beyond Rex's reach. "Give up while you can," Rex warned him.

The man didn't answer. He dodged down another branching tunnel.

Rex halted. This could go on a long while, if he followed the agile young man's route through the brush. He put his nose up, tracked his subject's progress. Then he stepped back through his memory to that overview he'd glimpsed. They were on a narrow section of a flat secondary terrace in Glen Haven Park. The thicket ran along one of the park's terrace walls. At the right end of it lay a muddy drainage groove; at the left end, a flight of steps.

The subject managed to keep his noise-making down to quiet

crackles of leaf and twig until at last he stopped deep inside the bushes. By now he'd probably put at least 15 meters of circuitous burrows between himself and Rex. Self-satisfied scent factors drifted out through the branches. He thought he'd escaped.

Rex snorted. Did he think Rex couldn't hear him breathing? Couldn't hear his heartbeat? Couldn't smell his bad self, over there by the terrace wall? Did he believe Rex could only follow his twisted path? Well, screw that. The subject was only four meters away if one took a direct route.

Rex sized up the tough bushes. This'd be doing it the hard way. But only for four meters.

He bunched his haunches, set his hind paws. Breathed in and out, and focused on his subject's location.

Then he launched himself through a blur of breaking branches with a roar.

His quarry screamed. He darted to Rex's left.

Rex rebounded off the wall, lunged after him. Twigs tore at him. He shoved through the brush. He reveled in the sweet taste of his subject's terror. He closed on the heat of his subject's body. Heard the frantic thunder of his subject's heart.

The man struggled free of the bushes. He sprinted upward, three stairs at a time. But no human could outrun an XK9 with a six-meter stride. Rex caught him in two bounds, clamped his jaws around the wrist of the EStee-hand, jerked his head, and laid his subject out on his belly on the landing.

The man gasped for breath. He stared at Rex's teeth on his arm, his scent factors raw with terror. A distinct, pungent odor of soiled pants rose from him. The young man dropped the EStee.

Rex raked it out of reach with a hind paw. Crappy substitute for a real gun, but illegal in civilian hands. Rex didn't fear it, but it could harm a human or an ozzirikkian, so he made sure the subject couldn't grab it.

"Backup's on the way," Charlie called. "Hold him!"

Rex growled. "He is not going anywhere!"

The subject whimpered.

Rex wagged his tail, but kept the man's wrist firmly between his teeth.

Crisp, warm satisfaction filled Uniformed Peace Officer Seaton's scent factors. "I have a DNA positive on our subject." She gestured toward the man Rex had flushed from the thicket and caught on the stairs. "Just as I thought! Meet Elmo Smart, AKA 'Thumper.' Got a rap sheet several klicks long. We've been trying to catch him for almost five weeks. He's been working this park and a couple of others, leaping out of hiding to mug unsuspecting passers-by."

Their captive, now cuffed in the back of a prisoner transport, sneered and looked away. But his bravado couldn't conceal the glum, sludgy dread in his scent.

Five weeks? Rex shot another look at the slender young man. That explained his familiarity with the terrain. "How many incidents?"

"In all?" Seaton's brows went up as if the question surprised her, then she frowned. "Oh, dozens. He's a one-man crime wave."

Elmo Smart was more dangerous than he looked. *That's two notorious thieves in one day.* Rex glanced toward Charlie, who'd stayed with Fatima and her friends. *Will we get any credit for that? Will 'the right people' know?* His partner hadn't yet had time even to pull out the traditional squeaky-toy. Rex kept his growl to himself, but that toy'd probably be the extent of the recognition he'd get. The play-reward practice dated back to the earliest days of K-9s on police forces, but the older Rex got, the more it felt like a mockery, not a reward.

Charlie seemed stung by this. *Dr. Ordovich always stressed it was important.*

Rex let a little of his growl out. *If you really want to reward me, let me spend time with Shady.*

Reluctance surged through the link. *I'm sorry.*

Rex knew Charlie's reaction was more than simple disinclination to subvert OPD protocols. Until about seven weeks ago, Charlie and Shady's partner Pam had been lovers. Then she'd dumped him, just a few days before the trip back to Rana Station. She'd left Charlie to take up with a former boyfriend, an OPD detective named Balchu Nowicki. *I can't really blame you for not wanting to see Pam. But Shady and I still love each other.*

Can we discuss this later, please?

Rex sighed. *You always say 'later,' but we never do.*

"Well, well." Seaton had continued perusing Smart's file. "Looks like we have a known human-exclusivist, here. At least, he's made some statements and boosted some posts in support. But an actual assault on an ozzirikkian is new."

Rex snapped his ears flat. "Probably because he never had any ozzirikkians to assault before."

Seaton's partner UPO Wells scowled. "Just needed to find one, I guess." He reached in to fasten Smart's seat belt.

Rex watched with close attention, growled a soft warning.

Smart rolled an eye at Rex. He behaved himself, but the sharp stink of his resentment hung in the air like an invisible fog, overlying his other smells.

Rex huffed. Resentment was probably Elmo Smart's normal outlook. Charlie said human-exclusivists lived on resentment. They ignored history to justify their bigotry, because without the ozzirikkians Rana Station never would've been financed or built.

Wells slammed the door of the prisoner transport, locking Smart inside. Rex rejoined his partner. They were on call later tonight. Charlie'd want to head home soon.

Paramedics were just finishing their examination of one of the ozzirikkians Smart had targeted. She clicked and whistled to her companion in their home language.

Rex couldn't make sense of what she said. New longing filled him. Shady was the Pack's linguist. She'd studied Pan-Ozzirikkian when she'd learned the Pack would come to Rana Station. If only he could ask her!

The paramedics gave both ozzirikkians pain-patches. They applied them to their foreheads. The blue-black patches blended in with the skin color of one better than the other, whose face was a lighter blue-gray. Soon the achey heat in their scents eased.

"Fatima, you remember my new partner, XK9 Rex Dieter-Nell," Charlie said.

Fatima smiled. She reached out a hand to Rex. "Who could forget? Hello and thank you. You really came to our rescue!"

Rex wagged his tail and offered his paw to shake. He let his tongue loll in a dog-smile. "It is my pleasure to remove someone from our park who would dare to threaten our neighbors and honored guests."

The two ozzirikkians had gone silent at Rex's approach. When he spoke, two pairs of round, violet eyes widened. Their heavy brows rose, forming wrinkles around their pain patches. They emitted sharp, brisk, rising scents that smelled similar to human amazement or surprise.

I'm always astonished by how many people are surprised that we XK9s talk.

He sensed Charlie's agreement through the link. *You're a new thing in their world. They don't know what to expect, so they assume you're a dog, except bigger.*

Kind of like the human-exclusivists talk as if ozzirikkians are some sort of Terrestrial ape?

Good point. Yes, very much like. Rex glimpsed Charlie's smile from the corner of his eye.

Rex turned toward the ozzirikkians with his ears up, tail waving. Both individuals had pale tufts of fur that partially concealed the two small, half-circle ears on each side of their round, furry heads. The tufts marked them as females. They'd wrapped their long, furry arms around each other. Like their elongated torsos and short legs, their arms were covered with thick fur, patterned in striking black, gray and yellow spotted markings. One had a vid-recorder on a length of webbing around her neck. Fatima turned to them. "Ter, Jik, this is XK9 Rex. He's Charlie's partner. Don't be afraid of him. He might *look* like a huge black wolf, but he's really very friendly."

The one with the vid-recorder loosened her grasp on the other, lifted her blunt, rounded muzzle and sniffed in short puffs through her flat, triangular nose. She cocked her head at him. Her alert violet gaze studied him.

He cocked his head at her in reply. "Hello."

Her flexible, gray-blue lips parted to give the long-toothed gape of greeting the Pack had been taught was a parallel expression to a human smile or a canine ears-relaxed tail-wag. "El-l-l-oh. T-tank you vor-r r-rezzgue us."

Her high-pitched voice spoke with studied deliberation, but Rex could follow her words. Shady said many ozzirikkians were able to create the sounds needed to speak Human Commercial Standard. It was much harder for humans to reproduce the clicks and squeaks of Pan-Ozzirikkian. Lucky for XK9s, their vocalizers could do both. Maybe he should learn at least a little Pan-Ozzirikkian from Shady. *If* he ever saw her again.

He wagged his tail, relaxed his ears. "You are most welcome."

"Please meet Terchikni Jochikti, Welder First Class," Fatima said. "She's the leader of my work-group."

Terchikni extended a hand that had six, slate-blue-skinned fingers with black, clawlike nails, an opposable thumb, and yellowish fur to her first knuckles. "My firzzt-t XK9."

Rex went to "parade sit," with head up, ears forward, and tail straight out behind. He offered his paw to shake. "My first ozzirikkian. Hello."

The ozzirikkian emitted high, bright scent factors that

smelled almost like excitement and curiosity in a human. "T-tiz XK9 so big! But-t very smart-t I t-tink!"

Rex let his tongue slide out in a dog-smile. He'd been hasty to think ozzirikkians were bizarre. This one seemed highly perceptive. "It is nice to meet you, Terchikni."

"And this is Jikjikchi Ziktikki, my partner from work," Fatima said.

Apparently emboldened by her work-group leader's example, but still smelling frightened, Jikjikchi also stretched out a hand to shake with Rex. "T-tank you," she said in a soft, high voice.

"And my longtime school friend, Nancy Tibma," Fatima added.

Nancy, a slender blonde human woman, smiled. "Fatima's told us about her XK9 neighbor, but I never imagined you'd come to our rescue." She reached up boldly to stroke his head and neck, then glanced back at Terchikni and Jikjikchi. "His fur is really very soft. You should feel it."

The two ozzirikkians hesitated, looked at Charlie.

Charlie grinned. "Rex loves being petted and admired. He looks fierce, but he's a lover."

Fatima and her friends encircled Rex. They stroked and caressed him, murmuring praise and delight. The ozzirikkians made contented little sounds deep in their throats, like a cross between a coo and a purr. Rex basked in their attention, tail wagging.

Charlie looked on, his brown eyes alight with pleasure. *See, you got to be at the center of admiration after all.*

Rex rolled over to let them rub his belly. *I definitely could get used to this.* All the same, no one had tried to pet Charlie, had they? Not Seaton or Wells, either. Humans were picky about where and when they allowed others to get near them. Yet everyone assumed Rex wouldn't mind if sapient creatures touched him wherever they liked. *Another form of condescension? Well, damn. Probably.* Then Terchikni's clever fingers found a really good spot. Rex sighed. *I'll worry about whether to be offended later.*

Charlie grinned. *Take your kudos where they come. Just don't expect me to lug your panniers up the switchbacks for you.*

Read the rest of <u>What's Bred in the Bone</u> from your favorite bookseller!

ABOUT THE AUTHOR

Jan S. Gephardt commutes daily between her home in Kansas City, USA, and Rana Station, a habitat space station the size of New York City, a very long way from Earth and several hundred years in the future.

Writer, artist, and longtime science fiction fan, Jan's been a teacher, a journalist, an illustrator, a graphic designer, an art director, a book designer, a marketing specialist, and an art agent, all while rearing two children and honing the writer's craft for several decades.

Her fine-art paper sculpture has been featured in regionally-exhibited one-person shows, juried into national exhibitions all over the United States, and is on display wherever she travels to science fiction conventions. She and her sister G. S. Norwood are the founders and co-owners of Weird Sisters Publishing LLC.

Read her blog, "Artdog Adventures," on her website.